UNCHIPPED:
ENYD

UNCHIPPED:
ENYD

TAYA DEVERE

DVm
PRESS

DVM Press
Vaakunatie 16 D 14
20780 Kaarina, Suomi-Finland
www.dvmpress.com
www.tayadevere.com

For information about special discounts available for bulk purchases, sales promotions, fund-raising and educational needs, contact sales@dvmpress.com

ISBN 978-952-7404-08-9 First Ebook Edition
ISBN 978-952-7404-09-6 First Print Edition

Cover Design © 2020 by Deranged Doctor Design -
www.derangeddoctordesign.com
Ebook formatting by Polgarus Studios – www.polgarusstudios.com
Editing by Christopher Scott Thompson and Lindsay Fara Kaplan

To all underdogs out there:
The black sheep, the odd ducks, the rejects, the loners.
You make this world go around.

ABOUT A GIRL

A short story in the world of the Unchipped series

Fifteen years. That's how long it took for her parents to give up on her. Hannah sits at the kitchen table and stares at the drained, weary woman across from her. The middle-aged woman's hand moves to the right, a vape pen pressed against her lower lip. The red lights on the AR-glasses blink as Hannah's mother looks as if she's staring straight at her daughter. Still, anyone who spent more than half an hour with this woman would know better: she's oblivious to Hannah's existence.

Hannah leans over the table toward her mother. "So, where are you sending me this time, Tricia?"

It's not surprising that her mother shows no sign of acknowledging her words. She's too far away from this reality. It's a small kitchen table, only two feet across. She's close enough for Hannah to see a few new gray hairs on the side of Tricia's French bob cut. But the table might as well be Hyde Park.

Only a year ago, calling her mother by her first name

would've been enough to pull the woman's mind from the charts and numbers and notes she's lost herself in. Tricia would have been livid. Unhinged. But a lot can happen in a year.

If Hannah's father were here, he'd give her a long speech about the new technology. How it's rotting everyone's brain, how the AR dooms humanity. Face-to-face meetings, another human's touch, a real connection... They'll all soon be extinct. At least, according to Fred.

Nothing like that will ever happen to Hannah and Benny. They won't be taken over by AR and turned into mindless robots or whatever it is this new future city is about to do. Though her father's right about her mother, that's for sure.

Despite the neighborhood gossip, Fred hasn't moved out, nor is he living in an institution somewhere. He's not dead, either. His slightly hunched back and dull gray business attire can be found somewhere in Europe. But rarely at home here in London.

"Fred's on a plane to St. Petersburg," his secretary Lidia would tell Hannah when she called her father's number. If she still called. The last time she did was on November 3rd 2086; a year and a half ago. She remembers the date because it was a day before her birthday. Hannah had hoped her call would help Fred remember the special day and send her CC's to spend at ShopDrop, the newest virtual reality mall just outside Holloway. But Fred never picked up his phone. He didn't send virtual coins either, just an e-card with teddy bears on it. Like Hannah was still six or seven years old. Maybe he thought she was.

"Fred's in the annual Helsinki meeting."

"Fred's traveling from Brussels to Berlin."

"I'm so sorry, dear, but the Wi-Fi on Fred's plane is down for security reasons. Would you like to leave a message?"

It's hard to keep up. So, Hannah doesn't. Her dad is gone more than he is around. And she can't blame him one bit. Who would want to live with a woman who stares into space eighteen hours a day?

Tricia takes off the AR-glasses. Hannah watches her blink as her eyes get used to the yellow kitchen light. Tricia lifts her gaze and scans the kitchen cupboards as if they're England's greatest miracle: something she's never seen before. Would her mind crack and shatter into pieces if Hannah were to introduce her to a steaming cup of black tea?

Once her brain recovers from the reality-gap, Tricia taps an address into her notepad on the table. She always keeps the notepad with her. It's one perk of her job as a city council member. She gets gadgets and the latest technology. Like she's someone important.

"Pfff…" Hannah rolls her eyes. Her gesture causes Tricia to abandon the notepad, where she's opened a map of London. *Just get on with your lecture, woman,* Hannah thinks. *I have pills to pop and people to do.*

"This is for your own good, Hannah," she says. "Things are changing."

"Oh, because you got Chipped, the world's a different place now? Guess what, Mummy-o? For the rest of us earthlings, the planet's still flat, and the sky is gray. Some of us still need to leave the house. But don't worry, I can take care of myself. You just dive into your new, blinking life. I don't need you or one of your stupid chips."

"Forget about the chip. That's not important. Just because I got one…" Her eyes wander back to the cupboards. Something there must be more fascinating than this conversation they're having for the umpteenth time.

Tricia's brow furrows. "How are they to fit us all in one city?" She seems to be talking to someone other than Hannah. "I don't care how many apartment complexes we're building. The numbers don't lie. There are too many of us."

Hannah waves her hand in front of Tricia's glassy eyes. "Ever heard of roommates? How about families and relatives living under the same roof? Isn't that what they used to do in America or Mumbai or one of those countries?"

"Mumbai is a city. Not a country."

"Whatever, Tricia."

Tricia leans her elbows on the kitchen table. Her long, boney fingers slide into her hair and stop at her temples. Locks of gray-black hair poke out. She looks electrified. "People need their privacy. Nobody's looking for a partner these days. They don't want kids. People want to live alone."

"Just like you and Fred."

Tricia sits back up and fixes her posture. Like road guideposts, two tresses of hair poke out on both sides of her oval-shaped head. "That's enough, Hannah. With all the 'Hannahs' you've pulled lately, I wouldn't bring your father into this conversation. Which news should I share with him first when he comes home?"

"If he comes—"

"Do I tell him about those repulsive photos? Or your lovely little drug habit?"

Fucking photos. Hannah's so tired of hearing about them. Why, oh *why* did she keep copies of her products? She should have just kept it all online. Keep the business going. Fill the orders. Take the pervs' money. Rake in the virtual coins, and call it a day. Who prints anything on actual paper anymore?

But she had wanted to show Benny. Maybe today she'll finally show them to him. It's time for her to nudge them out of the friend zone. Hannah wants him to see her in that light. As an adult. Striking and lusted after. A woman worth two hundred and forty coins per photo. Some days more.

How was she to know Tricia would go through her stuff while she was out ditching school?

Hannah leans back on her chair and crosses her arms on her chest. It's her turn to investigate the kitchen cupboards on the walls. "I told you already. Those pictures were just a joke."

"And who's laughing, Hannah?"

As tedious and tiresome as these mandatory lectures are, it's not the end of anything. Tricia makes the same threat every time. Hannah will be sent away. To a home. An institution. What did they used to call them? Do those things even exist anymore? Maybe out in the countryside or up in Ireland, they'd have a few left... *Boarding schools*? Yes, that's what they're called.

What a joke.

Three years. That's when Hannah will be of legal age. Old enough to leave London behind. To move away from these pathetic googly-eyed people who couldn't tell a real person from a hologram if it kicked them in their lady parts or dude-junk.

How is she supposed to grow up to be a decent human being? Of course she's into pornography. Why wouldn't she be mixing and matching pills, patches, and stickers? Hunting for the next high is the only useful thing to do. Fred's away three hundred days a year. Tricia plays a strange VIP in some augmented reality where they count numbers and stare at maps and talk about faucets and pipelines and wells. None of these people know how to touch or feel or care for anything but this new reality. Some new fucking miracle city.

Why would she wait? Everyone else around her is so far gone. She's the only one left in the here and now.

When Tricia is not working, she's shopping for yet another new, well-cut AR-suit. A world where you can become someone new in a matter of a few seconds and ten chip-credits. How is Hannah to compete with that?

Maybe that's why she tries new things. Things like taking naked pictures of herself and selling them online. Stealing and trying some of her mother's Happiness-Program pills. Just to see if they'd make her high or low.

But all they did was make her dizzy.

Tricia fingers the black edges of the AR-glasses. Are these few brief minutes outside her new reality giving her withdrawal symptoms?

"The place is called Kinship Care. It's just outside the city. Across the green hills, where we used to have picnics when you were a kid."

One picnic. We went out there once.

"And it's just for now, love. The people in charge of the chipping are about to solve overpopulation. But until they do, it's not safe for you to be here. I can't tell you more right now, it's classified."

Classified my ass, Hannah thinks, but instead of saying it out loud, she rolls her eyes.

"Once it's all done and dealt with, once the city is up and running at full capacity, I'll send the driver for you. You'll come home, get your chip, and we can all lead somewhat normal lives."

Hannah can't help but smirk. If she had a finger for every time Tricia's made this threat, Hannah could make a fortune. With that many fingers, she wouldn't even need to find a real alien for the perverts that keep asking her for "something with tentacles."

"Okay then. Green hills and Kinship kingdom it is. Here I come. What should I pack? And while I'm at it, should I toss Fred's stuff out your bedroom window and buy him a bus ticket so he can join me?"

After rubbing the bridge of her nose and smoothing her hair back, Tricia picks up the black glasses with the blinking red lights. "You're going, Hannah. Not because I want you to, but because if you stay in London, you're as good as dead."

"Little drastic, aren't we Trish?"

But her hands are already swiping up and down, left to right and back to left. She's gone back to sheets and diagrams and other things more intriguing than her self-destructive, boring teenage daughter. That's what she does, after all: escapes and ignores. And here Hannah thought that starting a million-coin business on the dark web would score her—if not praise and respect—then at least fifteen or twenty minutes of undivided attention.

Hannah gets up, grabs her jacket from the floor, and walks out of the kitchen. In the front hall mirror, she fixes her wild brown hair up in a ponytail. Benny would like to see the back of her long, fragile neck; she's sure most of them do. At least the ones who are not interested in aliens and their tentacles.

The city looks odd yet also familiar. The part of town where she grew up got the red glowing tiles later than the rest of London. Some buildings around her radiate warm air, some blink with an unnatural neon-red light.

The trees, bushes, and grass seem less green than they did before the augmented reality started to appear in Hannah's neck of the woods.

It's all so dull. While the rest of the world is ravaged by mass-deaths—people killing themselves or shooting into crowds—the United Kingdom languishes in an unbearable uncertainty of what's to come. Ever since the surgeons, nurses, researchers, and programmers who do the chipping arrived from the headquarters in Finland, the Happiness-Program has been available—to some. These people now call the UK by a different name: City of England.

Some people are against the program and the changes it will bring. Some people live for the change, for this new technology that will turn humans into machines—or partial machines. That's how Hannah understands it, anyway.

She's not against getting the brain implant. Her mother got it months ago, when her work won her a spot at the top of the list. She was one of the first people to go to the hospital for the procedure. Hannah's not excited about it either, though. She couldn't care less. Their pills won't give her the high she seeks, but they also won't harm her. Because she won't turn into her mother: sitting at the kitchen table working twenty-four-seven. No. She'll have the best of both worlds.

Anyway, the chip wouldn't be much different from the birth control capsule she got from the school nurse a year back. Any treatment, no matter if it's a shot or a pill or an implant, needs to enter your system—one way or another.

She takes a right from Abbey Road and continues toward the hospital. Her watch phone with a virtual assistant she's named Pingy, buzzes inside her jean pocket. "Read message," she says. Her mother would cringe at such ancient technology. But Pingy provides Hannah with all she needs.

Pingy beeps the tune she selected for Benny's messages.

AT THE ROOFTOP

"Answer message," she says. "Be there in five."

The front of the hospital glows neon-red. Multiple drones circle the building, delivering messages, medicine, and body parts from donors. Or that's what Hannah thinks they deliver.

Pingy plays Benny's jingle again.

CARTWHEELS OR CANDY?

Hannah waves her hand outside the hospital doors. Two sliding doors whoosh open. She darts inside and brings Pingy close to her face. Dodging the small self-driving scooters and buzzing drones, she half-whispers,

DEFINITELY DOTS

An elevator dings next to her, but to get where Hannah's going, only the stairs will do. The elevator's see-through walls would provide a clear view for any prying eyes. Not that anyone knows her here. But they know Benny. At the age of twenty-one, he's the youngest coder in the hospital.

10

She stops to look around. When she's sure that—much like her own mother—no one has acknowledged her existence, she pushes open the door to the staircase. Like so many times before, Hannah starts her long climb up to the top. On the fifth floor, she stops to catch her breath. Long brown curls dance around her face. She fixes her ponytail, then continues her climb.

At the top, she walks out onto the roof. The red circle in the middle of the roof is lit, glowing eerily in the weak sunlight. In the middle of the ring, Benny is kneeling down and investigating the ground. Hannah approaches him.

"You know you look like a complete nut-job, don't you?"

The man looks up. A boyish grin spreads across his face. Benny stands, his arms flailing above his head. "This must mean the city's almost set. I can't believe it's finally happening."

"For some of us, at least. Like you and my mother."

Benny turns to look at Hannah. The girl's annoyed expression wipes the grin off his face. With a few long strides, he's by her side. Hannah squeals as Benny grabs her, pulling her into his arms, lifting her up into the air.

"Well, I don't have my chip yet, Teddy," Benny says. He sets Hannah down and fixes the loose curls behind her ear. Is that more than a friendly gesture? Could it be? "But once I do, I'll hack the operating system and get you way the fuck up on the waiting list."

Hannah rolls her eyes but can't stop herself from

smiling. Would he do that? Would he care *that* much?

Benny starts toward the small shed behind the staircase entry. This is where the hospital keeps the drones that are not in service. This is where Hannah and Benny have had their secret meetings for five weeks now. And counting.

Benny taps on the electric pad by the door. The shed opens. The space was once used to store the hospital's helicopter. But now, hundreds of snoozing drones blink their little red lights, taking up all the wall and floor space. It looks like the night sky, but instead of twinkling, the stars are bleeding. Benny sits down on a pile of blankets and white pillows. Just a few of the items he's stolen from the hospital rooms downstairs. It's not that he's after blankets and pillows, but they need a place to consume the rest of the goods Benny's job provides them with.

Hannah sits down next to him. From his pockets, Benny digs out a handful of different-shaped pills and tablets. With his index finger, he goes through his stash. Then he shrugs and looks at Hannah, twisting his face like he's in sudden pain. "No dotties, Teddy. All I have is this 3D -printed bullshit."

Hannah sighs. "Whatever. I'll just order some." She taps the watch until an icon of a rosebud appears, brings Pingy to her mouth, and says, "LSD. Greater London." A short tone tells her the app is searching her keywords on three different sites on the dark web.

Benny stretches his legs in their self-made nook.

"Just let me pay this time. You always pay."

Hannah keeps her eyes on the search results on Pingy's screen but murmurs, "I make way more with my online business than you do working for the hospital."

He grunts at Hannah's words. "Speaking of, are you finally going to tell me what it is you're selling?"

Hannah doesn't answer. She fingers the folded photo in the pocket of her hoodie. Why does this happen to her? Why does he make her so nervous? None of the others do, her customers. Tongue-tied and nervous, Hannah shakes her head for no.

"Just say the word," Benny says. "I'll get you something in the hospital. And not some entry-level shit. A good job."

She doesn't mean the *pfff* sound escaping her mouth to be so demeaning, but it loosens her tongue. "And be stuck inside staring at numbers and code for four days a week? Surrounded by old farts and mad scientists, lusting for my brain? Thanks, but no thanks."

"It would boost your rank on the waitlist."

"Like I said, I'm good." Still staring at her wrist, waiting for the order to finalize, Hannah reaches for her pocket and begins to pull out the piece of photo paper. When Benny nudges her playfully, she quickly shoves it back into her pocket. It's not a change of heart. It's nerves. What if he laughs at her? What if he finds her disgusting?

"Whatever you say, Teddy." Benny nods up to the sky, visible through the open shed door. "I'll be damned. Doesn't it seem the deliveries are getting quicker each time?"

The low hum of a black drone surrounds them. As the small machine hovers above the red glowing circle in the middle of the roof and drops a small black plastic bag in the middle, Benny chuckles. "Who knew that the first augmented reality delivery the hospital would ever get is crystal tea in a biodegradable shit bag?"

When Pingy beeps twice, she gets up and leaves the cozy shed. She walks into the middle of the circle. The red light reflects against her clothing and her fair skin, turning her wild curls from brown to red. The light emits warmth and something else Hannah can't put her finger on. Once she's picked up the delivery, she spreads her arms and spins around. Benny laughs but doesn't come out of the shed.

"Come on, Teddy. I only have an hour before the graveyard shift begins."

Reluctant to leave the satisfaction she gets from dancing in the neon-red glow, she steps away from the light. Back inside the shed, she sits down next to Benny. He opens the poop bag, takes out two stickers with a rosebud on them. Before he hands the other sticker to Hannah, he leans back to investigate her face.

"Understand that you're way too young for this crap. You know this, right?"

Hannah reaches for the LSD sticker, but Benny moves it and the bag behind his back. "You're only fifteen. I looked you up today."

Anger boils up under Hannah's skin. In her pocket, she crumples the picture into a small paper ball in her fist. "Yeah, well," she says, unsure how to finish that thought. Tears burn her eyes. She's not sure if they're tears of disappointment or anger. Benny would never touch her. Not that way.

Hannah leans against the drones. "Doesn't matter. It looks like my mom's sending me away for a while, anyway. It's unlikely the drones will deliver where I'm going. I'll need to quit this stuff cold turkey."

"Why is she sending you away?"

"Something about it not being safe in the city for those who aren't chipped."

"How so?"

"I don't know. She said there's too many people or something like that."

"Too many?"

"Like, overpopulation."

"Oh. And what does that have to do with the chipping and AR?"

"Beats me."

"And do you believe that?"

"What?"

"That there's something fishy going on with the chipping? I mean, your mother would know about it. Maybe you should listen to her. What else did she say?"

Hannah dodges Benny's gaze. The last thing she wants is to talk about her mother. By her pink-gray sneaker, a small spider zigzags over, around, and under the hospital drones. As she reaches for the spider, it sprints and disappears into the pile of flickering machines. Shouldn't their batteries run out at some point? She wants to ask Benny but is afraid he'll think she wants to change the subject of their conversation. Which she does.

Hannah picks up a white drone. Her thumbs play with the metal propeller.

"I don't believe her." She tosses the white drone on top of a dozen others just like it. "Besides, I'm not going anywhere for a while. Might not happen at all. Mom's all bark but no bite."

"And the city being in danger?"

"She's overreacting, as usual. If those people in her precious new reality told her that Tom Thumb is a real-life boy, Tricia would rush to shop for a dollhouse and Barbie clothes."

"Which one was Tom Thumb again? A sin eater?"

"Who the fuck knows, Benny," Hannah says. Her tone of voice is too harsh, but she doesn't care. This is not how this meeting was supposed to go. Not what they're supposed to be talking about right now. *Doing*, right now.

Flustered and suddenly famished, she nods at Benny's hostage—the poop bag full of goodies. "Let's just get on with it. I still paid for it, so it's technically mine."

Benny sighs and mumbles something about jailbait. Hannah pretends she didn't hear it and keeps her eyes on her order. While Benny opens the black bag, he says, "Just out of curiosity. If you don't believe in your mother, and you don't believe in sin or fairy tales... What do you believe in?" His long fingers pick out two stickers. He places one of them on Hannah's tongue, one on his own.

Hannah closes her eyes and lets go. She gives up on all of it. Her hopes of getting Benny to lust after her. Her mother ever treating her as anything other than an afterthought. Screw them both. Screw this town. She stands up in the low shed.

"I believe I need to make things happen for myself. That no one else is ever going to have my back. Not my mother. Not some midget, giant, the devil, or God." Hannah snatches the bag from Benny and stumbles out of the shed. "*That's* what I believe in."

Waiting to come down from her trip, Hannah wanders the city streets. Old technology and buildings mix in with the new, neon-red scenery. It's hard for her to know what is a product of the sticker and what's a new addition to the ever-changing city landscape.

Billboards and AR-signs cast long shadows on the concrete streets next to the snaking tile road meant for the Chipped only. Hannah might walk on it one day, or she may not. Right now, small drones in all the colors of the rainbow march on the tiles' shiny surface. They stop near one another, and lift a small antenna, as if to greet their fellow drones. When two drones with spidery legs crash into each other, one humping the other, Hannah knows the little creatures are part of her feel-good trip. She chuckles and kneels down next to the tiles. High-fiving imaginary, fucking drone spiders is a first. She can't wait to tell Benny all about it tomorrow.

As she continues her stroll next to the red tiles, she stops in front of one of the 3D hologram displays that line up everywhere around the tiled road. They will soon reflect previously unknown AR-creations that hundreds of London's graphic designers have drawn over the past year. Digital pets, playgrounds, flash-fiction on billboards, 3D printed food, and goods. That's all her mother talks about whenever she's willing to put aside her new reality and focus on the old, boring one. The one Hannah and her absent father still live in.

The sun has nearly set. Hovering just outside the street where she lives, Hannah turns around and gazes toward downtown. If the streetlights, now reflecting glitter, were just the slightest bit brighter, she would be able to see a slice of the hospital's rooftop from here. The outlines of new buildings and old buildings, some blinking red, some standing dead in their gray frames, waver and change shape. A clutter of orange spiders slides across the neon-blue sky. They're all heading toward the green and yellow smoke that rises from a small shed on top of the city's largest hospital. Benny's hospital.

She's not ready to go home yet.

Hannah sits down on a fluffy pile of hospital pillows. They appear conveniently out of nowhere on the side of the two roads that circle around the endless row of houses. As she grazes her hand against the ground, the green grass turns into boiling water. She laughs at the bubbles as they burst one by one, leaving behind a glimmering puddle. In the middle, hundreds of ants carry around chips that are ten times the size of their little bodies. Hannah leans down, hoping to help them get the chips from one side of the puddle ocean to another. But as she reaches for the chip, it turns into a tiny puff of smoke, along with the worker ant carrying it.

She looks back up and searches for the yellow-green smoke. For the hospital. For Benny. But the sun has set, and darkness surrounds the blinking city lights.

The sound of car tires reaches her ears. Around the corner, a black van speeds down the road. It heads toward her street, toward the house where her mother will be working late, a set of AR-glasses glued onto her tired face.

Hannah gets up from the ground. As she takes a step away from her temporary resting place, the pillows and ants and chips all fade away. She looks up, and the city rises red and gray, new and old, make-believe and real. Hannah closes her eyes and takes a deep breath. She wants to get home. Tricia won't notice her state of mind. She hardly notices her existence at all.

She walks by the red tiles, wondering what their surface

would feel like under her sneakers. Though it's not forbidden to walk on the tiled road, it's created for those integrated with the operating system—the Happiness-Program. Hannah hasn't seen anyone walk on the road yet. Not even her mother, who's now able to see the adverts, the holograms, and the promises of a better tomorrow.

But that's because her mother barely leaves the house these days. The 3D printer she got from the city as her chipping gift turned out to be the only thing she still needed to become a total hermit. All the contacts, all the information she needs are in the augmented reality she's now a part of.

Hannah walks on a small sidewalk in the middle of the glowing tile road. The narrow pass way made with old fashioned red bricks is there for those who aren't integrated with the augmented reality. Tricia says the road will soon have "unwanted side effects" for those without the chip. That it could zap them, drain them. Hurt them. But her mother says a lot of things. Most of them she forgets as soon as the black-and-red AR-glasses go back on, covering the dark bags under her eyes.

As Hannah gets closer to home, she sees the black van again. It's parked in the driveway of her house. There shouldn't be any deliveries coming tonight. The food printer was filled just the other day, and the cleaning crew won't come for another five. No one needs new clothes or has scheduled medical checkups. All of Tricia's work files transfer through the operating system. Her whole life happens there. She wouldn't leave the house for anything.

As half of the van morphs into a familiar-looking shed and then back into its vehicle shape, Hannah curses the drugs in her system. Something tells her she should stay sharp. That something's about to happen.

She grabs onto her wrist. "What's the time?" she says and waits for Pingy to reply.

TWENTY-ONE-HUNDRED

Nine o'clock at night. Why would anyone visit the house at this hour?

She makes her way to the van. As she runs her fingers along the sliding door, a narrow, neon-blue line runs around the handle. Before she can think about what she's doing, Hannah pulls the handle and lets the door slide open with a *whoosh*. Leaning in, she closes her eyes and forces her brain to function right. No time for blinking spiders or brain-implant carrying ants now. She needs to find out what's going on.

She opens her eyes. The dim light inside the back of the van makes it hard to see. She leans deeper in. At the front of the space, there is a set of leather seats that look like they belong in a gaming room, not a van. Beside the seats, a low-set gurney. Beside the gurney, a pile of AR-glasses blinking neon-blue light instead of the usual red. On the wall, an electric pad shows a folder marked "Hannah D." She places her palms against the van's flooring and leans closer to read the smaller print.

"Hannah D. Unsuitable for H.P." She holds her

breath, watching as the letters turn into a stream of red blood. They fall against the pad's cracked screen and down the van's wall. On the floor, a white drone with a miniature mop cleans the puddle of blood.

She shakes her head, giving herself a small chuckle. "Get it together, Teddy," she tells herself.

Just as she's about to turn around and go find Tricia, the ground disappears from underneath her sneakers. Her body is now horizontal, supported by warm hands that hold her shoulders and her ankles, something cold pressed against the small of her back. Hannah moves her head from side to side, trying to see the force that has captured her—that now pushes her into the van.

An unnatural fog appears out of nowhere. A row of small spiders, ants, teddy bears, and tiny Bennys sit in the front yard, staring at her with big, wide cartoon eyes. One of the Bennys cocks his head and lifts a hand. A greeting. A small drone hovers above his head. The tiny cargo hatch opens and releases a dog turd that lands and squashes mini-Benny underneath its weight. Hannah chuckles and waves back.

"She's not going under. Sometimes other chemicals in the system may reduce the sedatives' effectiveness. Is your daughter under the influence of some substance we should know about?"

Now lying on top of the gurney, Hannah turns her head toward the unfamiliar voice. Tricia rubs the back of her neck, staring at the van, then back at the old woman dressed in red prison-guard coveralls. The hems of her trouser legs are too short, revealing a pair of swollen ankles.

"I wouldn't be surprised if she had taken something. At this point, I hardly know her at all."

"And you're sure she can't be integrated with the program? Doctor Solomon is said to be a miracle worker." Chubby-Ankles steps closer to Tricia. Lowing her voice, she adds, "And there's always the Chip-Center."

Tricia shakes her head. Her palms raised, she says, "That's not an option. Hannah may be a lost cause, but I won't turn her into a prisoner. No. Take her to Kinship Care. Maybe the discipline will do her more good than predicted." She lowers her hands and shrugs. "Not that I'm holding my breath."

The older woman nods at Tricia. She winces as she puts on AR-glasses with red blinking lights and makes a call. Tricia turns around and makes a beeline back into the house. Without looking back, she clicks open the front door and goes inside. The door *whooshes* shut behind her.

Hannah blinks, trying to tell if her mother abandoning her happened in this reality or her own reality. Which one is this?

She relaxes her head against the small pillow set on the gurney. White and flat. Just like the ones Benny brought to the shed, one by one. Stealing from those who won't be needing them any longer. The chipping is supposed to cure everyone's sickness. No more patients, no more viruses, bacteria, or unnecessary deaths. Are the Chipped capable of dying at all?

Before the van door closes, the little creatures hop on board. One by one. Like bleeding, blinking stars on a rooftop. Red coveralls lean over her. A cold sensation spreads around Hannah's back. When the van's motor purrs to life, the woman with big ankles moves toward the leather seats. On the first seat, just by Hannah's head, the little spiders, ants, teddies, and dog shit-covered Bennys dance around, hopping and sprinting. Her index finger pointing at the seat, she murmurs, "Not there. That seat. Is taken."

The woman stops and turns to see what Hannah is pointing at. Then she sits down on the next seat over and sets a box of something on a briefcase under the seats. Hannah moves her head and stares at the ceiling. Hundreds of rosebuds open into flowers. In all the colors of the rainbow, they form a glowing, neon field. The little creatures climb the walls of the van. One by one, they hop onto the field. There they continue their happy-dance, upside down but not falling.

"Just like. Tom Thumb…"

"What's that? You believe in fairy tales like that? At the age of fifteen?"

Eyelids heavy as a million drones, Hannah gives into the fog that has followed them from the front of the house she grew up in. "I don't believe… in… anything."

"Well, you're in luck, my child," the woman says

and bangs on the wall. As the van backs out into traffic, the gurney seems to Hannah to swing side to side like a lopsided drone. "We'll fix that in no time."

3

ENYD

January 2089
East-Land, City of England

CHAPTER 1
THE CLOSET

The beeping sound is muffled and distant, but she can hear it easily in midnight's silence. Fingers. Tapping. On a digital keyboard, something no one in this house should have access to. The rubber bottoms of her slippers thump against the wall-to-wall carpeting of the children's home.

Enyd looks up and stares at a camera on the wall, the one above the staircase.

"Come on, you piece of turd…"

But the AI refuses to talk. Instead, the camera turns silently on its axle until its lens points at a closed closet door at the end of the upstairs hallway.

"Was that so hard, Arnie?"

Enyd supports herself against the creaking railing. A step at a time, she creeps toward the cleaning closet. On the broad expanse of cinderblock wall above the stairs, a gigantic message board displays red glowing numbers.

950 739 CC

The number has never hovered this close to one

million chip credits before. Not during Enyd's time in charge of the charity program.

All the bedroom doors are shut. A blue light pierces the gap between the door of the cleaning closet and the carpet just outside it. The beeping continues. Once Enyd gets as close as two feet away, she hears the tapping of small fingers against the keyboard of a device.

How does the child not know how to turn the sound off?

Maybe because the children haven't had access to any devices for the past two years. For some, it's been longer. But Enyd already knows who is hiding in the closet. Only one of the children is bold enough to sneak into her office, break into the locked drawers, go through the seized goods, and steal forbidden electronics. Once again.

Enyd reaches for the door handle. Her short, swollen fingers pull the door open. There, among the mops, buckets, brushes, and dusting mitts, sits a teenage girl. The girl's purple-yellow fingernails now frozen on the smart phone's cracked screen. Ava. Kinship Care's only kid with a chip in her brain. But she's Unchipped—like Enyd.

As Enyd rubs the bridge of her nose, Ava hides the stolen device behind her back. In horror, the girl's wide blue eyes stare at Enyd's slippers. "Sister Enyd, I didn't know…"

The old woman steps forward. "Didn't know what? That it's wrong to steal? Or that lying about it only makes things worse for you?"

Ava's chin sinks to her chest. "Arnie didn't see me. Nobody did."

"Oh, but someone *did* see. Someone above."

Ava sits there, glaring at her. Biting her cheek. Holding her tongue, doing what she can to stop herself from lashing out. Enyd sighs and holds out her hand. "When lust has conceived, it gives birth to…"

The phone clanks against the closet's wooden floorboards. Ava wraps her arms around her legs and rocks back and forth.

"Ava? It gives birth *to*?"

The girl clears her throat. The hatred in her gaze prompts Enyd to stand taller. She won't fold. She won't show leniency. She can't.

"It gives birth to sin," Ava says.

Enyd steps forward, her hand outstretched. "And when sin is accomplished, it brings forth…"

Ava closes her eyes. She fumbles for the fallen phone. When she finds it, Ava holds onto it with both hands. Was she able to reach anyone outside the children's home? Would she know how to enter the Chip-Network?

Enyd peeks over her shoulder. The AI-camera points straight at them, its red light blinking: Arnie's recording. There's no turning back now. Enyd couldn't save the girl from what's to come—even if she wanted to.

Frowning, Ava looks up. Knuckles white, she holds the phone in her hands and presses it against her pajama top. "But it's my phone."

If this had happened last year, the girl would have already thrown a fit. Without a moment of hesitation, she would've woken all fifty-seven children sleeping peacefully in the twelve bedrooms upstairs, as well as the sixty kids sleeping downstairs.

Tonight, Ava won't throw a fit.

Tonight she knows better.

"Ava? It brings—"

With shaking fingers, Ava hands Enyd the stolen smartphone. Under Ava's long-sleeved PJ top, Enyd spots a blue and yellow bruise by the girl's elbow. One of many, she knows.

"Well?"

"When sin is accomplished, it brings forth death."

Enyd shoves the phone into the pocket of her robe. "Anything else this time?"

Shaking her head, Ava's eyes shoot daggers at Enyd.

"Just the phone, then?"

A nod is all Enyd gets. The girl's surely afraid of her guardian, but the early teen rage is rooted deep. She was twelve when she first arrived in the City of England and Kinship Care. Now that she's fourteen, Ava's pig-headedness and unpredictable behavior have finally cracked under Enyd's handling.

Hands clenched into fists, Ava stands up in the closet. "You can't keep me here forever. It's against my human rights."

Enyd scoffs and stares into the girl's piercing blue eyes. "Your *rights*? Oh, my sweet girl. It's a war zone out there. Chemical weapons, gas masks, and stray bullets. And here you are, tucked under a warm duvet, eating nutritious food. Yet, you're still complaining. Would you really rather be out there? Hunted? Dying?"

Ava scratches her shaved head. Even in the hallway's dim nightlight, the scar at the back of her skull looks irritated and red. Has she been digging for her chip again? In her sleep? The nightmares, the girl screaming until everyone else wakes up—that's the least of the trouble Ava has caused in this house. It's the most common reason for these nightly encounters, but it's not the bad dreams that get Ava bashed and bruised.

"I'll go back to the Chip-Center. I can live there."

Enyd chuckles and shakes her head. "And do what? Stumble on corpses? Eat half-rotten vegan-nuggets?" The soles of her slippers squeak as Enyd steps aside and gestures for Ava to come out of the closet. Hesitating, the girl steps into the hallway. She then quickly continues to her bedroom door, hoping to join her three roommates sleeping peacefully, oblivious to this nightly adventure. Ava reaches for the doorknob.

"Not so fast."

The girl's blackened fingernails hover on the doorknob. She could open the door and close it behind her. Hide under her bed or in the shared closet. Just like she has so many times before.

But Enyd would find her. Drag her back to where the cameras can see.

Ava turns around. Her bruised fingers fiddle against

one another. Slippers thump as Enyd walks toward the staircase and stops. She points her finger at a carpetless spot on the floor. The camera follows Ava as she slowly makes her way to the old woman.

Enyd nods at the floor. "You know what to do."

Ava gets down on all fours. Her voice shivers as she begins. "Forgive me, Father. Forgive me, Sister Enyd. For I have sinned."

Enyd steps forward. The front of her slipper hovers above Ava's index finger, pressed against the hallway's wooden floor. Enyd supports herself against the stairway's wooden railing and steps on Ava's finger. Her hundred-and-eighty pounds roll on top of Ava's already black bruises, as Enyd steps on her fingers.

She doesn't cry out. That would wake up the rest of the house and cost her five extra fingertips.

Enyd moves her foot to hover above Ava's middle finger. "Please free me from my sins…" The railing creaks as she again supports herself against it and lands her weight on the second finger. "…for the wages of sin is death."

The slipper moves onto Ava's thumb. Then onto her ring and pinkie fingers. The girl holds her breath and sobs silently between the applications of crushing weight. When Enyd pulls her foot away, Ava sighs out all the air in her lungs. She's about to get up, but Enyd's words make her freeze on the floor.

"And your wrist."

The girl shakes her head, doesn't look up.

"Well, maybe next time you'll think twice and skip your nightly adventure. Your wrist."

Ava lies down on her back, arm stretched out at her side. Enyd places her foot against the girl's wrist and steps on it hard. This time Ava can't help but squeal. With her free hand, she reaches for the front of her pajama top, shoves the fabric in her mouth to muffle her cry.

Enyd steps back and crosses her arms against her chest. Lips pressed into a thin line, she stares at the whimpering girl. Why can't she just be like the others?

The stolen phone beeps in the pocket of her robe. Ava winces at the sound but remains motionless, her eyes closed, and her face smudged with tears.

Heavy steps slowly pass her crushed hand and continue toward the stairs. The blinking AI-camera stays on Ava, who's now silently counting to a hundred.

Enyd starts to make her way down the stairs. "Make sure to lift those sleeves all the way up, Ava." She stops at the third stair but doesn't turn to look at the weeping girl. "Blissful dreams. May God forgive your lawlessness."

The sound of the hot-air system humming in her ears, Enyd struggles to fall asleep. She tosses and turns under the blankets, fluffs the pillow once again, and shoves her hands under her armpits to keep herself warm.

How is it this cold?

Oliver and Thomas must have forgotten to fill the

brick furnace in the cellar before they went to bed. Gardening, maintenance, and carrying water from the well in Kinship's front yard. That's what the boys are responsible for these days, now that the only things that need to be guarded are the rooms inside the Kinship Care. No one has tried to enter the premises for over a year. Safe and isolated. That's what the children have become. Just like Enyd always planned and wanted.

It's past midnight. Ava's latest crime has left Enyd too restless to sleep. She's tempted to tap the only other adult in the house. Or maybe she should walk across the hallway and knock on Margaret's door?

Margaret. You up? You forgot to lock the office door. Again.

Though the deaf woman infuriates her most of the time, Margaret's also the closest thing to a friend Enyd has these days. The boys, Oliver and Thomas, are hardly grownups; they just turned twenty last year. Both look like fully grown men. With their broad shoulders and sturdy frames, it's easy for them to tend to physical labor day in and day out.

Enyd's sure the two of them eat more than all the children put together.

A steady pressure starts at the back of her head.

"Margaret?" As soon as she says her name, Enyd senses who it is tapping her. A man. Reverend Dragan Marić.

"Grace and bliss, sister Enyd."

"And you, Reverend."

"I'm surprised to find you up so late. Margaret is sound asleep. As she should be. What keeps you from sleep, Sister Enyd?"

Should she tell the man about Ava? Would he even care? The reverend doesn't know what they do to the children. What it is that keeps the charity money coming in. He just wants to hear the numbers. His eyes lust for the red digits on the billboard above the staircase. But Enyd knows that if he learned the truth about the recordings, it would push Marić off a mental ledge. He simply doesn't have the stomach for it.

"Oh, just the old furnace. Frightfully cold here tonight. Lord knows I'm grateful for a roof overhead. But it would be nice if it wasn't collapsing."

The Reverend chuckles at her words.

"You're right. Many pray for such a safe haven. But with this month's numbers, I wouldn't be surprised if you had a hefty bonus coming your way. How does the CC score look tonight?"

Of course, he's calling about the numbers. Revenue—that's all he cares about.

Enyd sits up and kicks on the rubber-soled slippers. The AI-camera at the corner of her room comes to life. A blinking red light follows her as she walks to the window and peers out between its metal bars. The moonlight pierces the dark clouds. Kinship Care's high metal fence rises in the distance, surrounding the twenty-acre premises. The front gate is closed with a CS-key that only Enyd can open.

The last thing her predecessors did was to build that fence higher. So high that those looking for asylum wouldn't be able to climb over. But today, there's no one left to try breaking and entering. The plague took the sinners before they could even look for a place to hide.

Enyd's fingers wander along the window's metal bars. The cold, rough surface reminds her of Samuel. Of before.

"We're fifty thousand short of hitting one million CC's."

"Excellent work, Sister Enyd. God rewards the true believers. Keep up the good work. And please inform me when we have seven figures on the billboard, would you? I believe a celebration is in order, one way or the other."

"You'll be the first to know, Reverend."

Enyd examines her short fingernails in the dim moonlight. She is listening, waiting. The connection is finally gone. The reverend has decided to let her be.

On the bureau by the window, a white, plastic-covered bible glows in the dim moonlight. Prayer beads circle around a stapler, three pencils, and a yellow-paged notebook. Enyd sits down on the wooden stool by the bureau. She spreads the fingers of her right hand wide on the table and reaches for the stapler.

Ava's long and slender body, her blue eyes, and shaved blonde hair flash through Enyd's mind.

The stapler's top presses gently against Enyd's index finger. She swallows painfully. Enyd stares at the stapler, at her finger pinched between its hammer and the crimp area.

She thinks of the words she's learned by heart. The phrases, the meanings behind them. This would all be so much easier if she could find a way to fully believe in it.

"It's not up to me. It's God's will."

She presses on the stapler harder.

"I refuse to feel guilty for doing God's work."

When a sharp pain digs into her index finger, she pulls her hand back. Suddenly out of breath, Enyd nudges the stapler off the bureau. It lands on the floor by her slippers. The immense threat of pain has drained all the energy out of her.

The dining hall fills with the sound of a hundred and eighteen children's spoons clinking against porcelain bowls. A set of twenty AI-cameras follow kids of all ages as they eat oatmeal. A smaller billboard rises at the back of the room.

953 263 CC

The AI called Arnie has made a new video of Ava's injuries. Enyd curses at the moderate increase in numbers. A girl should bring in more CC's. Is Ava too old for the donors? Or is she old news altogether?

Enyd focuses on her task: finding breakfast. She does her best to ignore the nagging pain around her ankles as she limps into the kitchen. Margaret, Oliver, and

Thomas are opening cabinets, drying dishes, and stacking away plates and glasses and cutlery.

Enyd sits at the round table in the middle of the cooking area. She nods at Margaret, who then brings her a steaming bowl of porridge and a jar of strawberry jam. Enyd opens the lid and checks for dots of mold.

"This the last jar, Sister Margaret?"

The AI's voice replies before Margaret has a chance.

I COUNT ZERO JAM JARS IN THE PANTRY

"Thanks, Arnie," Enyd says. "Not that I asked you."

Margaret doesn't turn to look at Enyd. She's probably annoyed with Enyd for calling her "Sister." But rules are rules. Especially when the cameras are on.

The pressure at the back of Enyd's skull tells her the deaf woman would rather answer her telepathically than speak out loud. She always does. If it's because of Arnie, or because of her unique way of speaking, Enyd doesn't know. Margaret pronounces her words with care—in a shattered, particular way. She's always been a woman of few words, even before a rare illness caused Margaret to lose her hearing, first a little and then completely. But when she does speak, those around listen to her carefully pronounced words with undivided attention. The emphasis and authority of her voice is something Enyd secretly finds intimidating and troublesome.

Enyd lowers her eyes and sinks the spoon into her porridge. *And how low are we on bread?*

"Twenty loaves. In the. Freezer."

And sacks of oats?

"I opened. The last one. Yesterday. Morning."

Enyd looks around the kitchen. The people who control the AI, those ordering videos of bruised, supposedly sick children, always demand more whenever they send in a food order.

"Make them look more banged up," they'd say. Or, "Can you have yellow pus coming out of the wounds?" followed by, "Can we have a younger plague victim this time?"

But they all have to eat, don't they? What options does Enyd have?

Ava got into the phones again, Enyd tells Margaret silently. *Last night after bedtime. I think Arnie already sent in the newest video material.*

The deaf woman continues washing dishes and doesn't answer Enyd. Talking about the videos makes her practically mute. She refuses to take part in that part of her job. It's solely due to Enyd's efforts that the charity program does so well.

I'll make a food order after breakfast. Let's hope that last night's video was enough.

"And if. It isn't? What if. They want more? If fingernails. And arms. Aren't. Enough now?"

Enyd rubs the bridge of her nose. Margaret. The food order. Her sleepless night. It's all starting to give her a severe headache. *I'll take care of it, Margaret.*

"Until. What? What do. They have to. Ask. Before you. Say. That's. Enough?"

Oliver walks over, interrupting their silent conversation.

He carries a small plate of Finnish crispbread and a handful of raisins. Enyd eyes the plate, then Oliver. Her brows rise in a question.

"We're almost out of tea, Sister Enyd," Oliver says. He sits down next to Enyd and nods toward the food he's brought her. As she has done so many times before, Enyd wonders whether the wooden chair will hold the boy's weight. But Oliver seems oblivious to the seat struggling under his broad frame.

"Plenty of this stuff left, though." He picks up a piece of crispbread and sniffs it. "Too bad it tastes like cardboard."

Margaret turns around and walks to the already-dried dishes by the cupboards and starts loading them in. Enyd fishes out a chocolate granola bar that she shoved in her pocket the day before. Under the table, she nudges it against Oliver's leg. The boy takes the bar, shoves it inside his sleeve. Before Enyd talks, she glances at the kitchen's AI-camera. The lens points at Margaret by the sink but then starts zooming out to see the whole kitchen.

Enyd gives Oliver a half-smile. Her voice booming, she says, "We should thank the Lord for having anything to eat at all, Oliver."

Oliver's brown eyes meet Enyd's. He smiles and nods at her. "Oh, I am. Very grateful." He then reaches for one of the crispbreads and takes a bite. A steady scrunching sound fills the kitchen.

Enyd turns her focus back to her oatmeal. She takes

a spoonful while Oliver finishes the rest of the bread. Her pockets may be empty now, but she has plenty of granola bars left, back in the office. A woman her age and size can't possibly survive with this tasteless nutrition... the porridge, the bread.

Thomas joins them at the table. Before he sits down, he steals a few of the raisins from the plate between Enyd and Oliver. Enyd glares at him but doesn't say a word. She's not a fan of the raisins either.

The two young men are continually testing her limits. Their endless appetites—them and the rest of the teenage boys living in Kinship Care—force Enyd to order food more often than she'd like to. It puts her deeper into debt, a debt her soul despises.

Oliver grabs the rest of the raisins. Margaret stares into space, drying an already dried plate. Thomas hums a familiar tune, a jingle from the time before. Something feels off. Is it because the sun is out this morning? Most days, the playground's brownish grass looks like the blood from The Great Affliction ruined it only yesterday—not two years ago.

"What's on the agenda today, Sister Enyd?" Oliver asks, his mouth full of porridge. How has he not yet retreated into a dark corner somewhere to devour his secret treat? The boy has more self-control than Enyd gives him credit for.

Thomas crosses his elbows on the table and leans forward. "Maybe we could take Margaret for a long walk after breakfast. She hasn't been out for days."

The boy's sarcastic. Margaret doesn't need people to walk her. Though she does tend to lock herself in her room and stay there for most of the day. Only Arnie knows what happens behind that closed door.

Enyd looks up at the dish-washing woman. Margaret doesn't say a word. Not out loud or inside Enyd's head. The boys can't talk telepathically. Margaret and Enyd are the only Unchipped living in the home. Margaret, Enyd—and Ava.

Ignoring the sarcasm, Enyd says, "That sounds like a wonderful idea. Why don't you walk to the southern fence and take a look at the green hills again? But don't take too long. I need to make a new food order today."

She doesn't have to say out loud what that most likely means. Work-wise.

"What's up with you and the hills? Do you think there's a new batch of survivors?" Thomas asks. His eyes flicker with enthusiasm. It doesn't take a lot for the boys to get excited these days. Not much happens around Kinship Care. Except when a sinner is caught red-handed.

"Enyd thinks she saw a body," Oliver says.

"Whoa. A human body?"

Oliver nods repeatedly. "Yup. The drones must have collected it before we had a chance to see it."

Why is there disappointment in Oliver's voice? Why is he so eager to see dead people?

"That's quite enough, boys. Just check the hill. Not for bodies, or drones, or anything specific. No need to make a fuss about everything all the time."

A careful knock on the door cuts their conversation short. Enyd turns in her seat. Hannah—a girl with curly brown hair tied in a ponytail—twists her hands and approaches Enyd with lowered eyes. A sweater three sizes too large covers her upper and midbody, all the way to her knees. She's one of the older girls, soon turning seventeen. Enyd can't help but check the girl's fingertips. Nails bitten to the quick, but no bruising, not as of late. Hannah had been one of the toughest kids to handle when she first arrived at Kinship Care. A few weeks down in the basement had done her good. Enyd knew it would, but she was surprised when the girl seemed to have turned from a full-on rebel to a shy and sheepish girl—almost overnight.

Margaret hurries over to Hannah. She leans forward and whispers something in Hannah's ear. The girl nods. Margaret walks to the cupboard, takes out a clean bowl, and fills it with porridge. Then she walks back to Hannah. The girl's hands shake slightly as she accepts the bowl, her eyes flicking nervously to the AI-camera, then to Enyd.

Enyd leans back in her chair. Behind Hannah's saggy sweater, another Kinship Care tenant hovers nearby. When Noah's eyes meet Enyd's, he quickly looks away and pretends to have found something interesting to read on the kitchen's bulletin board. The boy's about a year older than Hannah. One, two, three, *four* bruised fingertips.

Has he sent the girl to beg for more food? It's a known fact that Enyd favors those who give her and the rest of the adults less trouble. She's not known for giving out seconds. But Margaret is.

Again, Margaret whispers in Hannah's ear and then ushers her out of the kitchen.

Enyd leans back and pushes her bowl away. Why did she have to give Oliver the only granola bar she brought with her? Eating her treats without the others noticing is challenging, but she's become quite good at it. She knows how to hide, even from Arnie.

"What was that about?" she asks, frowning at Margaret. The woman dodges her piercing gaze and turns to finish the dishes. Oliver and Thomas exchange a look. Enyd stares them down and nods at the AI-camera. The boys get up at once.

"Arnie, gather the kids. Prepare the playground cameras for an outing."

Thomas and Oliver follow Arnie's smooth voice into the dining hall. Enyd and Margaret are left alone in the kitchen.

Grunting, Enyd limps toward the sink. Her ankles always give her the most trouble after sitting down. Enyd places her bowl on the counter. Margaret has been drying the same bowl since Hannah left the room.

"Scrub any longer, and that bowl's going to become see-through."

Enyd reaches for the dish brush and runs water on her hands. A few pumps of soap and she starts cleaning the porridge bowl with force. The food order has put her on edge. Without looking at Margaret, she continues with a low voice.

"Why do you let that boy pull your leg like that?"

"What. Boy?"

"Don't tell me you didn't see Noah hovering by the bulletin board."

"They were. Just. Hungry."

"They're all hungry, Margaret. And the older boys already get a bigger portion of each meal. Hannah must weigh, what? Ten or eleven stone? She shouldn't beg for him."

Margaret lowers her chin and closes her eyes. Enyd tries to read her mind, but she's blocked the connection. She's not answering Enyd's tapping. She reaches for the dishcloth in Margaret's hand. After taking the rag from her, Enyd puts it down next to the bowl and turns Margaret by her shoulders. The two women face each other in the quiet kitchen.

With a low voice, Enyd leans in and says, "I know you and I don't always see eye to eye. On many things that need to happen around here. But if we start hiding things, keeping things from each other, the order here will turn into chaos. Do you think the Lord would want that for the children? That I'd want that? Is that what *you* want?"

Margaret's eyes fill with tears, darting from one of Enyd's stern brown eyes to the other. The pressure at the back of Enyd's skull tells her the connection's open again.

"She's with. Child. Hannah."

Enyd lets go of Margaret's shoulders. "You mean one of the youngsters? Did they break something? Steal? Sneak out?" Enyd cocks her head and keeps investigating Margaret's desperate expression. "What then? What did she do?"

"No. Not the. Youngsters. A child." Margaret lowers her chin. The light-brown curls dance around her beautifully aged face. When she looks up, she glances at the AI-camera, then her serious eyes stare at Enyd.

"A baby."

The office chair creaks lightly under Enyd's weight. She's triple-checked that both doors, the one leading to the library and the one to the downstairs hallway, are appropriately locked. She can't have anyone witness the AR-call she's about to make. Not even Margaret.

Biting into her fifth chocolate chip granola bar, Enyd hauls herself to her feet and walks to the window. With her free hand, she moves the heavy drape aside. It's midday, but the curtains are drawn, blocking the dim daylight from outside. The office's three windows open to the north, where the City of England glows red. Today's weak sunshine makes the city more visible than most days even though it's a great distance away.

A group of five young children runs past the windows, chasing a football. They sprint all the way to the broken statue of a rearing horse by the front gates.

From there, they turn back and chase the ball toward a goal made of two red traffic cones. Their giggles are loud, and they holler at each other as they go. Enyd lets the drape fall back down. With heavy, awkward steps, she heads straight back to the office chair and a note placed in the middle of the desk.

The food order.

The wooden drawer opens halfway, then gets stuck on its slides. Enyd nudges the drawer sideways, pushes it back a few inches, then pulls again. It opens without further trouble. Chocolate chip, red berry, and peanut butter granola bars fill the deep drawer. Enyd sinks her hand into the depths of her secret stash. She pulls out a warm can of root beer. The can makes a hissing sound as it opens.

Enyd plunges her hand back in. In the middle of the pile, her fingers find a set of black AR-glasses with blinking red lights. The other pair is buried deeper, unused and pointless. No one else is allowed to touch this technology. Just Enyd.

A sacrifice. For the greater good. To keep everyone alive, Enyd must play along.

After taking a big gulp of root beer, she lifts up the AR-glasses. They make her wince when they reach her eye-level. The red lights create a throbbing headache that starts from her left temple and stops at the back of her skull.

It's God's punishment. For I have sinned, she thinks to herself. But nobody's tapping her and Arnie can't read her mind. There's no need to pretend. Religion is just something to control the kids with, to make them behave as they should. And it's working like the lucky charms the Chipped in the cities are known to be so fond of.

Bright, blinking colors greet her eyes. Images fill the screen and fill her mind as well.

A glowing, red hologram of a fit woman running by the shore.

An old but well-tuned man jumps into a pool.

3D printed pills, shaped like American footballs.

A smooth woman's voice—a female Arnie—describing the Happiness-Pill 2.2, now available for everyone in the Happiness-Program.

"Arnie. Make this damn thing call Nurse Saarinen. City of Finland."

CALL INITIATED

Three white dots run across the colorful trailer. Soon, a slightly nasal voice with a thick accent booms in Enyd's ears.

"Ahh, Enyd. About time you called. You must have, what, a half a sack of oats left?"

"Good day, Nurse Saarinen. Yes, we're running on fumes here. I would like to place an order, please."

"I'm sure you would. Go ahead. Ready when you are."

Enyd raises her brows but reaches for the note on the desk. Usually, Nurse Saarinen barters before asking for the list. This is a good sign. Ava's video might have been payment enough.

She wipes her hands on the front of her pants and reaches for a pair of reading glasses. If she lived in the city, they would have fixed her eyesight a long time ago. Just like they would have fixed Margaret's hearing.

"Fifteen sacks of oats. Two bags of sugar and salt. Each."

"Would rye be okay? Half and half?"

Enyd takes a deep breath and closes her eyes. How she despises these calls. To be the one compromising, not the one calling the shots. She's here to keep everyone and everything in control, not the other way around.

"We'll take whatever you have, Sister Saarinen."

"Nurse."

"Yes, of course. Nurse Saarinen. We'll also need tea, flour, honey, and sanitary products. The usual amounts."

"The boys into baking now?"

"Sister Margaret is."

The woman scoffs at the other end of the line. After taking a moment to write down Enyd's order, she says, "Tell you what. Though these calls are recorded, you can drop the act with me. Religion died long before The Great Affliction. Must be a drag to keep up with such superstitious fairytales."

"Aren't people in the City of Finland carrying rabbit feet in their pockets?" Before Nurse Saarinen has a chance to reply, Enyd says, "People need something to believe in. If they don't trust something bigger than themselves, they have nothing. It gives them hope."

"I prefer clarity over hope. A clear understanding of

what people must do. Your children need to stay in Kinship Care, and the rest of us must stay in the cities. How else are we to protect them from the plague, or the war—or themselves?"

Enyd reaches for the glasses, pulling them off her skin by just one inch. The throbbing around her skull does not lessen. She doesn't feel like debating humanity's future with the nurse. Enyd presses her lips into a hard line.

Nurse Saarinen continues. "Surely, you'll want the usual package of root beer, granola, and cupcakes, too?"

Enyd looks at the half-full can of root beer longingly. As soon as this AR-call is done and dealt with, she'll empty the can and open a new one. Have a vanilla cupcake or two.

"That would be great, yes. The kids love sweets. Personally, I like to stick to the porridge." As soon as the lie comes out of her mouth, Enyd regrets it. Arnie makes sure nothing that happens in this house ever stays a secret.

"Whatever floats your boat, Enyd. What else do you have on your list?"

"Twenty-five packages of black tea. Fourteen boxes of powdered milk. Five sacks of black and kidney beans. All the flour you have to spare. Same with strawberry jam, honey, nuts and seeds, pasta, and frozen goods." Enyd puts away the list. "And a package of blockers with better syringes this time."

"You need more crispbread?"

Enyd shakes her head and stops herself from rolling her eyes. Not because she thinks the nurse could tell, but because the gesture would only make the piercing headache worse. "We're all set with crispbread. Thank you."

"I'll toss a few packages in anyway. We've also got some vegan nuggets and soy slices leftover from a party they threw in the Pedal-Center. I'll make sure they're sent your way as well."

"Thank you, Nurse Saarinen. That will be all."

Enyd reaches for the AR-glasses, her whole body itching to shove the device back into its hiding place and secure it with a double lock.

"Not so fast, Enyd. We need to talk about donations."

Enyd cups her ears and rubs the sides of her head. The pain has started to numb the skin around her ears. "Arnie got new material just last night. I figured we'd have at least a few weeks until you ran out of clips. The girl's pretty bruised up. What more do you need?"

"Well, that's exactly what we need. *More*. We also need face shots. People need to see that this plague is ruining more than just wrists and fingertips. That it's not safe outside the city. Not with the murderous Unchipped running loose and a deadly virus wiping out what's left."

Margaret had seen this coming. Enyd supposed she had seen it coming too. They would always ask for more. More shocking material. More pain. More punishment. Suffering, starving, hopeless people. Those who dared to defy the Happiness-Program. It's just that no one in Kinship Care is one of those people. Not in reality. Only on camera.

"Also, Doctor Solomon has requested material of younger children."

Enyd presses her knuckles against her temples. "How young are we talking?"

"I'd say six and down. And we need more…realistic material. Not just black eyes and fingertips. Something more shocking. Blood, rotting wounds, missing legs. We need to really show the good people in the city what it's like for those who defy the program."

"I'm sorry. *Missing legs?*"

"You get the gist."

Enyd's eyes find a stapler, just like the one on her bedroom's writing desk next to the white Bible. Her heart misses a beat when she imagines Owena or any of her other five-year-olds covered in blood and bruises. The videos are for the greater good—their only way to survive—but she wouldn't be able to punish the little ones. Unless they broke the rules. Maybe then.

"Why not take pictures of the real plague victims?"

"Oh, Enyd. They're long gone. You and the children are the only people left in the City of England. The rest of the cities are in lockdown because of the Unchipped uprising."

"Then send the airship to get us. Send a helicopter. A plane."

"You know we can't do that. It's just not safe to

move you. Besides, with the revenue your charity program is bringing in, operation Kinship is way too valuable to be shut down."

"What about if you just took the shots and—"

"Photomanipulation won't work. People are not stupid, Enyd. We need real tears. Real blood."

Enyd grabs the stapler and holds it hard in her fist. A suffocating lump rises in her throat. What would Margaret do? She would fight this. Stand up for the kids. She'd find a way to stop this madness.

"Do you want the damn food or not?"

Enyd lowers her chin. She lets the stapler drop back onto the table. In the screen of her AR-glasses, a young woman wearing a revealing bathing suit surfs along perfect waves. Behind her, the letters "H.P." glow in all rainbow colors. Happiness-Program. It's for everyone. *As long as you're carrying an undamaged chip in your head,* she thinks.

Someone has to feed the kids. Guide them. Keep them safe. Until they can be brought back into civilization. Are these atrocities really worth starving for?

"Please send the Chip-Ship as soon as possible. Like I said, we're on our last sack of oats."

"And the new material?"

Again, Enyd reaches for the stapler on the desk. With her finger shoved between the hammer and the crimp area, she weighs her options. The boys wouldn't beat the five-year-olds; Enyd refuses to believe anything else. And even if they did, Margaret wouldn't let them. As much as Enyd hates to admit it, her power over them is limited. She needs to sacrifice someone else to get the food. A real sinner.

"Maybe we don't need the young ones. What if I got something much better?"

Enyd can nearly hear Nurse Saarinen frowning as she waits for her to elaborate.

"How does a seventeen-year-old pregnant girl sound? Would that boost the donations?"

CHAPTER 2
THE LONDON EYE

She taps her knuckles against the wooden door. A young girl calls out for her to come in. Kinship Care used to have a no-closed-doors policy. But Enyd quickly learned that the less time the children spend together without supervision, the better. And with only four adults under one roof and over a hundred children and teens, supervision is a limited resource.

Enyd opens the door and steps in. Two bunk beds on each side of the small room hold four girls. The youngest—Owena, five years old—gets up and abandons her book. The girl's big for her age, strong too. She's known to wrestle with the older boys, sometimes winning and leaving them puzzled by her strength. Owena makes a beeline for Enyd and takes her hand. "Sister Enyd, can you read to me?"

Enyd squeezes Owena's shoulders. "Not right now, my child. I need to have a word with Ava." She stands up and looks around the room. "How about you go pick out a new storybook from the library. Once you're back, I'll read the first chapter to you."

Marie and Sarah, both ten years old, jump out of bed and hurry to the door. Owena claps her hands together and jumps on the spot. As the three girls bound out of the room, Enyd hollers after them, "No running! If you see Sister Margaret, or Brother Oliver or Thomas, let them know I sent you. And just go to the library and back. No detours!"

Enyd closes the door behind her. Ava sits on a bottom bunk bed, her arms hugging her long legs. She's wearing winter gloves, maybe because it's still chilly inside. Maybe she's hiding the consequences of her recent theft.

When Enyd gets closer, Ava's whole body starts to tremble. Is it out of fear—or rage?

Ava looks up and says, "Sister Margaret said she'd give me my shot later."

"Oh, I'm not here because of your diabetes, Ava." Enyd sits down on the wooden stool by the writing desk between the bunkbeds. "I'm here because we need to talk about what happened last night." Enyd nods at Ava's gloved hands. "Wearing gloves is not going wipe away your sins."

The girl hesitates but then pulls the gloves off. Ava twists her hands as she hides her black fingertips and closes them inside her fists. "You've already punished me for those sins."

"I know I did, my child. But something tells me you

don't regret what you did. Not really."

Ava's eyes drill into Enyd's. "It's *my* phone. My mother bought it for me. It belongs to me. Not you, or anyone else."

Enyd leans forward on the chair. She reaches for Ava's hand and squeezes it between hers. "Even so. Who are you to call? Your mother is gone, Ava. They're all gone. What use is that phone to you at this stage of life? What were you doing with it anyway?"

Ava pulls her hand away. She hugs her legs tighter and buries her head between her knees while Enyd reaches for the reddened skin of an infected wound on her head. She's surprised when the girl doesn't shy away from her touch. "You're having nightmares again?"

She doesn't reply.

Enyd gets up and digs around in her pockets. A small bottle of alcohol in one hand and a clean tissue in the other, she sits down on the bunk bed next to Ava. Carefully she cleans the dried blood around the wound. Ava doesn't wince, though Enyd knows the antiseptic stings. The girl's tougher than most.

"I don't think my mother is dead." Ava stays bundled into herself. Enyd's hands stop for a split second. Then she pours more alcohol on the tissue and finishes cleaning the wound. As soon as she's ready, she reaches for Ava's chin and lifts it up so she can see her watery eyes.

"Oh, my child. Just because she's not on earth any longer doesn't mean she's not with you. Your mother's

59

watching over you every single day. One day you'll meet again. You'll just need to work to earn your place in heaven until that day comes. But enough with these shenanigans. Smartphones and hacking into the Chip-Net. You're better than that."

Ava's eyes become stern suddenly, wiping out her look of desperation and sorrow. Her eyes dart between Enyd and the AI-camera. She lowers her voice and hisses, "But I don't have to hack anything. I just open the browser, and the phone connects. If you let me use the phone for just fifteen minutes, maybe half an hour—"

"Absolutely not. You can't trust the information you find on the Chip-Network. A lot of it is taken over by the rebels. Fake, hearsay... all lies."

Ava leans closer to whisper. "But I know she's out there. I found a picture of her. Pedaling an electric bicycle in a blue city. That's the City of Finland, isn't it Enyd? If my mother's out there, she can help..."

"That's enough." Enyd stands up and shoves the alcohol back into her pockets. "For fools speak folly, their hearts are bent on evil..."

Ava jumps up from the bed, screaming, "I don't give a fuck about your devil! Or your Jesus! Your evil spirits and angels are just a bunch of bullshit!"

The piercing sound startles them both: Owena, crying. Enyd turns to see that the girls have returned from the library. Marie holds a thick storybook with an Abominable Snowman on its cover. Sarah kneels down and wraps her arms around Owena.

Ava hurries to Owena. "Shit, shit, shit." She kneels down to pet the crying girl's head. "I'm so sorry, Owena. I didn't mean to yell that way. Or say those nasty words. I didn't know you were back already. It's okay. It's all good."

But the little girl cries even harder. Enyd gets up from the bunkbed and walks over, shoving Ava aside. With one hand, she grabs the little girl's shoulder gently. With the other hand, she lifts up the crying girl's chin, fixing her posture.

"There, there. You'll be okay. You know why, my child? Hmm?" Enyd nods toward Ava, gathering her breath, kneeling down a few feet away.

Enyd clears her throat and smiles. "Because you would never do such things. Say such words. You would never sin, my love. Not the way Ava has."

Owena sobs quietly but stands an inch taller. Rubbing her eye, she turns to look at Ava, then turns back to stare into Enyd's eyes. "What did she do, Sister Enyd?"

"From the fruit in the garden of Eden. To machines that control minds."

"What does that mean?"

"She stole something."

"What did she steal?"

"The devil's device. Something that lovers of self, lovers of earthly temptations, and proud, arrogant, abusive, and disobedient children seek. Tell me,

Owena," Enyd glances at Ava, "Do you know what a smartphone is?"

The little girl has stopped crying. She pouts and sniffs, her fist glimmering with wiped tears. "A thing from our past. A reminder."

"That's right. And what do they remind us of?"

"That we must stand against evil."

"And would you ever touch one of these phones?"

"Or AR-glasses," Ava murmurs quietly. As Enyd's cold gaze pins Ava's mouth shut, the teenage girl crosses her arms on her lap. Her gaze wanders around the room.

"I wouldn't touch one. No."

"And why is that?"

"Because anyone who does is possessed by Satan."

"That's right, my child. You'd know such a person is a devil in disguise. Now, if you ever see someone with one of those devices, you know what to do. Don't you, Owena?"

The little girl's eyes widen. Her mouth makes a small letter O. Her nod is nearly invisible, but it leaves a stern look on her round face. A wrathful look. She'd know what to do with the devil. She knows not to bend and break in front of evil. She'd put an end to it.

"Good."

Enyd gets up and shoves her hands deep into her pockets. With a few slow steps, she makes her way to the hallway. One nod and the rest of the girls hurry back into their bedroom. Ava looks up and blinks rapidly. "Sister Enyd, I didn't mean to say those things."

Enyd stares down Ava. Her face is calm.

Panic rises on the girl's face.

"Enyd, please. I didn't mean it."

Lips pressed into a hard line, the old woman keeps staring. The girls in the room hold their breath.

After a gesturing nod from Enyd, Sarah hurries to a shared wardrobe. Then she walks to Ava, carrying a small, red fabric bag. Everyone who lives in Kinship Care knows what's inside: a change of clothes, two red blankets, and a small travel pillow. All the children have a bag identical to this one. And they all pray they'll never need to take it out of the closet.

Sarah drops the bag next to Ava. With a weak voice, she says, "Out of the same mouth come praise and cursing. My sister, this should not be."

Tears running down her face, Ava picks up the bag and stands up. Without looking at Sarah, or Owena, or anyone, she walks to the staircase. Her head hangs low. With resigned steps, Ava starts her way to the basement.

The heavy door creaks loudly as Ava pulls on it with both hands. The smell of mold and mouse nests tickles Enyd's nose. The smartphone burns against her hand, as she checks for the fifth time whether she's remembered to bring it with her. Her sweaty hand grips a box of blockers.

In a room right below, the furnace makes a whooshing sound as they continue toward the basement. The sound makes Ava stop and squeeze the red fabric bag against her chest.

"It's just the furnace, Ava. Keep going."

The girl is stalling. She turns and looks at Enyd pleadingly. "But I haven't got my shot yet, Sister Enyd. Maybe we should go back upstairs."

"No need." Enyd lifts the blockers in her hand. "I've got it right here. I'll do it once we're down there." Silently, she curses the bad-quality syringes the City of Finland keeps sending. Everything the drone ship drops on the premises is a second quality product: food, clothing, even medicine.

One careful step at a time, they walk further into the depths of Kinship Care. A steady pressure at the back of Enyd's head makes it hard for her to focus on the dimly lit stairs. Someone's tapping her. Margaret, she's sure. But Enyd doesn't have time for Margaret's protesting and pleading. What she's about to do is bad enough without the woman criticizing her every word and move. What's to come is inevitable.

It must be nice to be in Margaret's goody two shoes. Cooking, pampering, caring, and then reaping all the benefits the Chip-Charity has to offer. Kind and soft—that's how the children would describe Margaret. And Enyd? She doesn't need to know what the children think of her. Because at the end of each day, it does not matter. Cuddles and kisses on the forehead will never make the world go round. The CC's collected, that's what keeps them all fed, clothed, and alive. Enyd. That's who has to do the heavy lifting. And Enyd alone.

Enyd shakes her head and hopes Margaret will stop harassing her. For a second, Enyd doesn't look down, and her foot slips on a step. She loses her balance. One hand grabbing onto the metal railing, she's able to support herself well enough to land on her buttocks and stop her body weight from rolling down the steep stairs.

"Motherf…"

Enyd catches herself cursing just before Ava turns around. If the girl has heard her slip, she doesn't let on. Quickly she climbs the stairs that separate them and reaches for Enyd. But Enyd shoos her away.

"It's okay. I just slipped. I'm fine." Enyd pushes against the brick stairs, trying to get up. Stabbing pain in her ankle makes her give in and sit back down on the step. "You go ahead, Ava. I'll meet you down there."

The pressure around her temples worsens, forcing Enyd to hold her head. Blocking someone is not something she's used to doing. Ava doesn't know about the ability she has, and Margaret isn't what one would call a chatty personality. The reverend only checks in for the charity score once a week.

"Did you hit your head, Sister Enyd? Maybe we should get back…"

"It's just a headache, Ava. Now go. I just need a moment to collect my bones."

"But Enyd, I…"

A stern look is enough for Ava to swallow the rest of her objection. Pressing the red bag against her chest, she turns and continues down the dark stairway toward the basement room.

Enyd groans and reaches for her ankle. She rubs the joints gently, hoping a few minutes of rest will help her get going again. She could tap Margaret and ask for help, but then she'd need to tell her what happened.

But the pressure only gets worse. Annoyed and tired, Enyd opens the connection.

"Margaret, now is not a good time."

No reply. The deaf woman is slower than usual today. It happens. Usually after a new video, whether Margaret had to witness the bruising or not.

After a minute of silence, Enyd stops rubbing her ankle. She focuses on the person tapping her more closely; it's not Margaret, after all. It's not the reverend either. It's no one she's ever met or spoken with before.

"Who is this? Now is not a good—"

"You don't know me. Yet. But I think you know the person we're looking for."

Enyd doesn't know this woman, but she'd recognize the accent in her sleep. It immediately brings crispbreads and a blinking set of AR-glasses to her mind.

"Are you from the headquarters? One of Doctor Solomon's little Unchipped puppets? If this is about the donations, we've agreed all communication must happen through AR-calls, and they should be scheduled—"

"I know Laura Solomon, but I definitely don't work for her. Quite the opposite."

Enyd's frown deepens. She digs deeper into the

connection to see through the Unchipped eyes that tap her for the first time. A red glow reflects on buildings, billboards, and road tiles. She's surrounded by people. In a lit-up city. They're right by the old main street, where Enyd used to live. Before the tiles, before the world became restless.

This Unchipped woman is in the City of England. Right now. Walking. Talking. *Alive.*

"What is this? Who are you?"

"My name is Kaarina. I'm looking for a young girl, Ava. Her mother is—"

Enyd quickly blocks the connection. She sits in silence, stares into space. Ava has made her way down to the basement room, where she'll be spending the next seven days. Why are the rebels searching for Ava? How are they not dead? The woman, Kaarina, didn't wear a gasmask, nor did the people she travels with. Why isn't the deadly city killing them?

Dizzy and nauseated, Enyd closes her eyes. She must have seen something wrong. Has her damaged brain pulled a trick on her? She focuses on remembering what it was she saw through the Finnish rebel's eyes.

Red tiles zigzagging around concrete parks.

High buildings and fake trees with neon-red leaves.

Empty but lit billboards.

A blinking Ferris wheel: The London-Eye.

But something's missing. What?

She's heard of this woman. Nurse Saarinen has mentioned her several times during their AR-calls.

Kaarina—the Unchipped rebel who unbalanced the order of City of Finland, the Chipping headquarters. The uprising she started by recruiting a bunch of Chipped people to leave the city ended up stirring up cities all around the world. This chaos is the reason the plague videos are needed. Why Kinship Care still exists. Why Enyd is about to follow a teenage girl down to a basement where she will be punished for breaking the rules that Enyd came up with. All based on memorized phrases and sentences that Enyd has read in the white-covered Bible.

And now, the rebels have made their way to the City of England. Alive. Unharmed.

She shakes her head, forcing her shattering mind to focus on the task at hand. She pushes the thought out of her head, refusing to believe its possibility. She's too far gone, everything is. It's too late to turn back now.

With two hands on the railing, Enyd pulls herself up on the staircase. As she follows in Ava's footsteps down to the basement, the neon-red images keep flashing through her mind. She stops at the last step.

That's what's missing. That's why the main street looked so eerie and wrong.

No bodies on the roads.

No bodies by the London Eye.

No bodies in the plague-ravished city Enyd has been forced to run and hide from.

It's hard not to look at: the red blanket with a matching pillow, set in the corner of a cold and moldy basement room. The sound of the old furnace fills Enyd's ears. Water drips somewhere nearby, down the stone walls and onto the concrete flooring. Drip. Drip. Drip. Enyd presses her fingers around the box of blockers.

It's also hard not to look at the shivering girl. She stands by her cold hard bed, reluctant to sit down but too anxious to stand still, either. So she hovers, hugging her arms tight around her petite body.

"Time for your shot," Enyd says.

Ava turns around. The look on her face sends chills through Enyd's exhausted body. The girl could easily attack her. Run up the stairs and find Margaret. Start a little rebellion of her own. Just like that She-Devil, Kaarina.

But Ava rolls up the sleeve of her sweater. Slowly, she sits down on her red bed and reaches for the small travel pillow. She squeezes it against her chest like a teddy bear. The gesture makes Enyd wince.

It has to be done. For the greater good. For the children.

But her mantra doesn't ease the pressure rising in her chest.

While she places a clean needle into the syringe, she brings to mind something Reverend Marić once said to her. *As for you, you plotted evil against me, but God changed it into good. To bring it about that many people should be kept alive, as they are today.*

It's from the Bible. She's taken upon herself to

memorize as much of it as she can. Most of the time, when repeating what she's learned, Enyd doesn't know what the words actually mean. But Samuel had known. And he had never been wrong about a thing.

Her hands shake slightly as she pierces the rubber seal of the vial. Mockery. Pity. Abasement. That's what it means, when the City of Finland sends them this supply of second-rate materials. Kinship Care has never seen 3D printed band-aids, medicine capsules, or implants.

But devices like these wouldn't do. Samuel wouldn't have believed in using the devil's devices.

That's what she tells the children. That technology like that is unnatural, an invention of the sinful. It'd only turn them all into pathetic creatures, constantly seeking comfort and convenience. People whose lives are filled with vanity, turned away from anything that God created.

No. Being cut off from the outer world is better for the children. Anything that remains outside Kinship Care has no meaning, no value. The only danger remains outside the metal gates. Danger like deadly diseases, deadly weapons, murderous rebels. It doesn't matter why the Unchipped woman is looking for Ava. All that matters is keeping the children safe. Inside Kinship Care. Samuel's church. Under Enyd's control.

"Sister Enyd?"

Ava's words startle her. A few awkward steps take Enyd to the red blanket and the girl. She stands next to her bare arm. Whether it's her arthritis or her fall on the stairs that sends small spasms up her leg, she doesn't know.

With a slightly shaking hand, Enyd empties the syringe into Ava's arm. The girl looks away but doesn't wince or grimace. She's gotten used to the shots after two years of living in the home. Enyd gets up and puts the box away.

In her mind's eye, Enyd looks for Margaret. It takes a minute until the deaf woman answers her tapping. The connection opens, but Margaret doesn't greet her. Her silent ways drive Enyd to the brink of insanity. Careful not to speak out loud, Enyd turns away from Ava.

Margaret? Could you please bring Hannah down to the basement?

The silence continues.

Did you hear me? Can you—

"What. For. Sister."

Enyd sighs and sits down on the only furniture in the chilly room: a wobbly chair by the heavy wooden door. *Don't Sister me, Margaret. Just go get her. And tell Oliver and Thomas that the furnace needs attending. Tell them to meet me here after.*

Enyd waits while Margaret looks around the basement through her eyes. She can sense the panic rising in the woman's head. For a moment, Enyd's sure Margaret will resist. That she'll rise up against her leadership and command.

"I'll bring. Her. But I want. To stay. With the. Girls."

Enyd grows impatient and relieved at the same time. *When has that ever been a good idea? Your being here will only slow the process. Just bring the girl. And ask the boys to take Noah to the furnace room.*

"Noah? Why?"

You know why. He's a sinner, just like Hannah.

"You have. No proof that. He's the. Father. I think. They are. Just. Friends."

Could it be? Enyd thinks back over the two years they've spent in Kinship Care. Friendships aren't something she pays attention to. But the cafeteria is. Where does Hannah usually sit? With the other teenage girls? With youngsters? Images of antique dining tables and long wooden benches flash through her mind. In the farthest corner, far away from the kitchen, she sees Hannah and Noah. Sitting opposite one another, chit-chatting. Laughing. Next to them: Oliver and Thomas. Leaning over empty bowls of food. Relaxing. Off duty.

It doesn't matter what Enyd thinks. Or Margaret. The boys will know who the father is.

Fine. Just bring me the girl then. I'll deal with Noah later.

Enyd closes the connection, hoping that she has intimidated Margaret enough to do as she's told. If only the fragile woman could be as easy to handle as the boys are. Oliver and Thomas would never give her grief. They're too eager and thirsty for action. Willing to do anything to avoid another dreary, excitement-free day herding the children.

Enyd rubs the back of her neck as the pressure starts to build up again around her head.

Ava's suddenly by her side. "Sister Enyd, are you sure you didn't hit your head? You seem to be in a lot of pain."

Enyd has never realized how hard it is to pretend, to hide the conversations inside her head. But the girl can never find out. Not if Enyd wants to keep her safe. Alive.

"Go sit in the red corner, Ava. I'm fine." Enyd rubs the bridge of her nose. "I'm just… praying. We'll begin once we're all here. Until then, just leave me be."

Ava backs off. She walks back to her uncomfortable bed, sits down, and buries her head between her knees.

The connection opens again.

"Thomas. Wants to know. If he is. To bring. The rolling pins."

Footsteps echo from the stairway. The door to the furnace room opens. The sound of two sets of footsteps reaches her ears. Enyd hears a careful knock, then gets up and pulls the heavy door open. Wearing a bulky sweater that reaches her knees, Hannah walks in. She's carrying a red bag—identical to Ava's. She stops in the middle of the concrete floor, hesitating. It's not that she hasn't been here before. But she's never been here with another sinner joining her. Ava nods at the corner opposite hers. The girl, brown hair tied up in a messy

73

bun, walks to the corner. She starts spreading out what's inside the red bag, creating a bed like Ava's.

Margaret hovers by the doorway. Enyd walks over to her and lowers her voice. "You can go now. Doesn't do you any good to see this."

The woman won't meet Enyd's eyes. Margaret stares over Enyd's shoulder, to where the two girls shiver on the concrete floor.

Enyd clears her throat. "Sister Margaret. It's bedtime soon. You have over a hundred people to check up on. I've got this covered. We have no need for you here."

She lingers, reluctant to leave. Enyd places her hand on Margaret's shoulder and pushes her gently but firmly back toward the stairway. Finally, Margaret's shoulders slump. She turns and walks to the stairs. Slowly, one step at a time, she makes her way back upstairs.

Chatter echoes from the furnace room. Enyd waits for the boys to finish with the firewood. Once they walk out, Oliver takes off a pair of heavy-duty gloves and places them on a wooden bench by the furnace room door. Thomas raises his eyebrows at Enyd. When the old woman says nothing, he asks, "They both here?"

Enyd nods.

"And Noah?"

Enyd shakes her head. "I have some questions before we bring him down."

The boys exchange a look but don't say anything. They walk in, Oliver carrying a black duffel bag and Thomas cracking his knuckles. Enyd catches her breath when she sees their relaxed demeanor. Her fingers squeeze the smartphone in her pocket. Arnie doesn't see what happens in the basement. No one does. She'll need to use the smart phone's camera to record the video.

The heavy wooden door *thumps* shut. Suddenly dizzy and feeling drained, Enyd sits down on the chair beside the door.

The duffel bag is open on the floor. Both boys dig around in it, stopping to place items on the floor or to put on a pair of leather gloves. Three industrial metal rolling pins, each a different size, clink against the concrete floor as Oliver sets them in a neat row.

With a deep sigh, Enyd fishes the phone from her pocket. Her fingers shake as she enters the pin code into the device.

1-2-3-4

The phone makes a clicking sound. Bright blue light shines up into Enyd's face. She does her best to keep her expression blank. Like what's about to happen has no effect on her whatsoever.

Hannah has pulled the oversized sweater over her knees. Her back pressed against the stone wall, her wide eyes travel from the boys to Ava, and then back to Oliver and Thomas. No one says a word.

After a few minutes, the boys stand up and turn toward Enyd. They nod in sync. Then they fold their gloved hands and lower their gaze.

Enyd turns off the phone and shoves it back into her pocket. Then she stands up, folds her hands, and begins.

"Father, forgive them, for they know not what they do."

Ava and Hannah exchange a look. Ava folds her hands. Hannah follows her example.

Enyd continues, "And forgive us our debts, as we also have forgiven our debtors…" She clears her throat. The room spins slightly around her. "The Holy Spirit, whom the Father will send in my name, will teach you all things and will remind you of everything I have said to you. Peace I leave with you; my peace I give you. I do not give to you as the world gives. Do not let your hearts be troubled, and do not be afraid."

Enyd nods at Oliver. The young man walks to Ava, pulls her up from her red bed. He leads the girl to the middle of the floor. "Lie down, please." Ava lies down, her back against the floor. Enyd stares at the girl. Why can't she just stay out of her own way? Let go of the outside world, and what used to be?

She digs out the smartphone and taps on the video icon.

RECORD

The Chipped won't show this part. The work the boys do will never make it into the final video. But they will want proof of Enyd's methods. Evidence that she is still obeying their orders.

Enyd's voice booms against the stone walls. "Then, when lust has conceived, it gives birth to sin. And when sin is accomplished, it brings forth death."

Thomas picks up a rolling pin and walks over. He kneels next to Ava's arm, pushes the rolling pin against her flesh. His bodyweight drops on the pin.

Ava's scream makes Hannah curl up into a ball. A ball so small, the only thing Enyd sees is the oversized sweater: a woolly, shaking bundle. A pregnant bundle. She's a sinner. A reprobate.

In a way, she deserves this. Doesn't she?

Thomas works his way around Ava's body. Each time he kneels down and works the rolling pin, Ava's piercing scream makes Enyd close her eyes. The phone shakes slightly in Enyd's hands. Oliver's right fist lands on the side of Ava's left ear. Once the screaming ends, the boys pick the Unchipped girl up and drag her to the wooden chair.

Thomas goes to get Hannah.

Hannah doesn't fight Thomas, but he struggles to get her up from the floor and then lower her down to the middle of the floor. The girl's stomach is big enough for her to need help getting down. Thomas looks at Enyd, his eyes searching for something. A confirmation? Is there a small piece of him that doesn't want to go through with this?

"Sister Enyd, could you give me a hand? She's too… she struggles to get back down."

Enyd walks over. Gently, and with Thomas' assistance, she helps Hannah lie down on the floor. Before she can stop herself, Enyd's hand softly brushes the top of Hannah's head.

After five punches, Hannah's head lolls to its side.

"Stay away from her stomach area," Enyd says. Then

she hesitates and continues. "Let's only work on her left side today. And Oliver, that's enough with her face. It's supposed to look like the plague, not a boxing match."

"But last time you said—" At Enyd's stern look, Oliver shuts his mouth in the middle of his objection. Clearly agitated, he shrugs once and crosses his arms against his chest. Thomas picks up a rolling pin. Just as he's about to press Hannah's left arm between the pin and the concrete floor, Enyd takes a quick step forward. "Hold on a second."

From her pocket, she picks out the box of blockers. She takes out a clean needle and a syringe and prepares the shot as she's done a hundred times before. But this time, she doesn't know what the shot will do. The blockers are meant for the Unchipped, those with a broken implant in their brain. Not for one of the Chipless whose brains are chip-free.

Enyd struggles to find a vein in the girl's arm. Thomas digs out a flashlight. In the flickering yellow light, Enyd finally finds the vein and empties the syringe into Hannah's arm. The girl winces and muffles her scream when the needle pierces her skin.

They stand in silence and wait. After a few minutes, Enyd nods at Thomas. "Show me some light. I need to see her eyes." Thomas does as he's told. Hannah's eyes are blurry and unfocused. Just like Enyd hoped they would be. She's out of it. Her body's not used to the substance, so it's hitting her hard. Harder than it hits Ava.

"You can proceed now, Thomas."

Enyd walks back to Ava who nods in and out of consciousness. Enyd fishes out the smartphone. She sits on the floor beside Ava. Gently, she shakes the girl awake. "Sweetie. I need you to take off your sweatshirt and pants." As if in a dream, the girl obeys. She strips off the clothing she's wearing and puts on the red shorts and a tank top Enyd hands her from the red bag. Then Ava takes the second blanket and wraps it around her bruised body.

A dull *thud* tells Enyd Oliver is ready with Hannah.

With a deep sigh, Enyd points the smart phone's camera at Ava. The girl looks up, slightly less blurry-eyed, clearly in pain from the beating her body has just taken. Enyd reaches for the blanket and places it over the top of Ava's head. She arranges the fabric so that the blue bruising around her limbs shows up clearly along with her swollen face.

"Okay, Ava. Start counting."

Ava's eyes travel from the phone to Enyd and back. Finally, she nods.

"One. Two. Three. Four. Five…"

Enyd presses the video icon. She zooms in on Ava's injuries, her tear smudged face, and her body shaking from pain and cold.

"Twenty-one. Twenty-two. Twenty-three."

Enyd starts praying. This time—for the first time—silently.

Please, God. Let Nurse Saarinen approve these wounds

and bruises. Let Doctor Solomon's team make a video so overwhelming that none of the Chipped will ever dare to leave their city, ever again. Let these two plague-ravaged girls show them what waits for them outside. Help them understand how fortunate they are to live inside the Happiness-Program.

CHAPTER 3
2 YEARS EARLIER

The prison's TV room is empty, except for a lonely shadow sitting in front of the TV. His chin is lowered. The man's not really watching the telly, where a cheery woman chops vegetables for her weekly cooking show. The volume is turned all the way down, and the central heating's low hum is the only sound in the room.

Enyd's rubber-soled work slippers tap against the prison's concrete floor. A keychain with multiple USB sticks and keycards rattles to the rhythm of her steady step. She shouldn't be here, not without the guards shadowing her steps. But it's worth the risk. He is worth everything.

Enyd stops behind the bald, wide-shouldered man. His skin looks pale. Paler than it did the day before.

"Samuel…"

Enyd's voice creaks a bit and then fades away. By clearing her throat, she's asking for permission to join the prisoner. When it's just the two of them, a different set of rules applies. All the tables turn. It's the only time when Enyd's willing to lose all control. To be the one without the reins.

Samuel taps the plastic seat next to him. Enyd walks around the row of chairs and sits down next to the dark-skinned man. They've had these late-night chats so many times, but the tickling sensation in her stomach never seems to cease. It makes her feel as though she's a teenager—not a sixty-something-year-old prison counsellor waiting for her pension to kick in.

The man turns over the book he's been reading. A white, plastic-covered Bible. Smiling, Samuel turns to look at Enyd. "If I were a genie in a bottle. If you were to release me. What would be your one wish?"

Enyd can't help but smile back at the man. "A wish? That's what you're giving me?"

Samuel looks down at the Bible cover and shakes his head. "Greed is a bottomless pit."

Enyd can't help but chuckle. "And here I thought your Bible didn't have any room for superstitious things like genies and magical wishes."

"Nothing wrong with a bit of fun. Call it a brain teaser. The thought of the day."

Playfully, Enyd rolls her eyes. She folds her hands and relaxes against the uncomfortable seat. "Well, okay then. I wish…" Samuel reaches for her hand. A warm wave travels through Enyd's whole body. "I wish that I could find a cure. That I could go out there and heal those who have gotten sick. That I could make people stop hurting each other and hurting themselves. I wish I could take away their guns and pills and knives. Bring back the peace and order."

Samuel's thumb caresses the back of her palm. Enyd squeezes his hand, leaning closer. But only an inch. Someone could walk in at any minute.

"That's a big wish, Enyd. And hardly just *a wish*. Sounds more like a dozen of them."

"Call me a bottomless pit, then. But what else is there left to hope for?"

"Sounds like you've been watching the news again."

She nods. Holding on to his hand with both of hers. "It's bad, Samuel. More people dying. Hospitals too full. And useless anyway, as the doctors are now infected as well."

Samuel's calm expression doesn't change. A small smile lingers on his cracked lips. Enyd fights the temptation to touch his three-day beard. Deep in thought, he nods, the movement almost too slight for Enyd to notice. "They all have bruises? Swollen skin?"

"All the same. Their bodies rotting away. Faces turning to ash. Lungs too weak to breathe."

Enyd reaches for the Bible but keeps her eyes on Samuel. The man is too composed. Too tranquil. He should be trembling. Panicking. Bending under the sad fact that their world is coming to its end.

Enyd squeezes his hand tighter. She clears her throat and lowers her gaze. The plastic on the white Bible is stained and scratched. "Some people are talking about leaving the country."

"And where would they go?"

"Anywhere outside the United Kingdom. Warden Bailey fled to Finland. He was promised a brain chip and a house in the AR-City. Instead of preventing prison breaks, he'll be watching movies about them through these glasses. He'll have a whole new reality. Anyone with a chip will."

Samuel smirks and lets go of Enyd's hands, folding his on top of the Bible. "Whoever sows to please their flesh, from the flesh will reap destruction. Whoever sows to please the Spirit, from the Spirit will reap eternal life."

Enyd looks up to the television. The woman is dropping chopped-up vegetables into a boiling pot. Her expressions are too lively, too excited for her to be doing something so ordinary. *Cooking*, while an unknown sickness wipes out people outside the studio. But she isn't really in that studio. The show's a rerun, and the woman is already shipped away to wherever celebrities and rich people now live. Maybe somewhere in America? Enyd doesn't know.

"You want one of those chips. Don't you, Enyd?"

She's too afraid to look at him. Too scared to see judgment or criticism on his beautifully rough face. But she should know better; Samuel is beyond such things. His heart is full of warmth, love, and third chances. Every time Enyd is near him, she feels like a better person. She *is* a better person. Someone worthy.

She picks up the Bible and waves it in the air. "Is a chip against His will?"

Samuel smiles, but doesn't answer. He reaches for Enyd's hand, the one holding his Bible. When their fingers touch, Enyd holds her breath. The warm sensation travels from her stomach all around her body. Let them see. Let them walk into the room and witness this love.

His hands browse the Bible's thin pages. Enyd places her hands on her lap, unsure what to do with them. Not only does Samuel make her feel like a teenage girl, but he makes her act like one as well.

"All things are lawful for me. But not all things are helpful. I will not be enslaved by anything. But I refuse to tell you what to do, Enyd. It's not my place to do so."

They sit in silence while the spirited woman on the TV takes a first taste of the vegetable stew. When the hallway lights turn off for the nighttime count, Samuel reaches for Enyd's hand. When the rest of the prisoners return to their cells, the two sit in comfortable silence.

Hands folded. One mind at ease. One in turmoil.

The pain is almost unbearable. Enyd wakes up amidst beeping machines and devices. Unable to lift her head, she looks to her side to see a pair of feet, poking out from under a white hospital sheet.

A commotion behind her tells Enyd that someone has noticed her moving.

"Laura? Laura, we have one. One out of twelve. It's the old woman with ankle edema. She's almost awake."

Enyd blinks slowly. No matter how hard she tries to move, her head stays flat on the surface it rests on. A hospital bed? An operating table? She's not sure.

A voice with a thick Nordic accent fills her ears. It's pleasant—soothing—to hear the woman talk. But the feeling of losing control sends Enyd's pulse racing. The monitor next to her now beeps frantically.

"Enyd? Enyd, can you hear me?"

She opens her mouth to talk, but her throat is too dry. A woman in a white doctor's coat snaps her fingers. "Nurse Saarinen, could you get a glass of water? Remember, not the tap. Use what we brought over on the jet."

Soon Enyd feels a metal straw gently pressing against her lips. She drinks the water from the cup that the nurse is holding. When she sucks in air instead of water, the doctor gestures for the nurse to go get a refill.

"Enyd, dear. I'm Doctor Solomon. How are you feeling?"

Enyd smacks her lips together, clears her throat. "Is it done?"

Doctor Solomon reaches for Enyd's head and strokes her hair gently. Her touch is a weird contrast with the throbbing pain Enyd feels at the back of her skull. She wants to lift her hand and touch the bald patch on her head. But her arm is made of lead, her fingers sleeping soundly.

"Yes, dear. The chip is installed. The operation went well." The doctor reaches for Enyd's fingers, squeezes

86

them firmly between her warm hands. "But I'm afraid there was a complication."

Why is a woman nearly half her age calling her "dear"? It makes her feel even smaller. Even more out of control. Out of her comfort zone.

"A complication?" Enyd says, her voice raspy and weak. "What kind of a complication?"

"It's your chip, Enyd," the doctor says and smiles apologetically. "I'm afraid it's not firing properly."

"Firing?"

"That's right. The implant was installed successfully, but it's not integrating with the system."

Enyd swallows her annoyance and says, "So I can't go where he went?"

"I'm sorry, hon. But I don't quite understand."

"Warden Bailey. He left London and moved somewhere safe, and I was promised I could go too. I just need some time to convince... I need to get Samuel..." Enyd's voice fades away; the dryness in her throat causes too much pain. The nurse and the metal straw could not have returned at a better time.

Doctor Solomon lets Enyd drink in silence. She turns and puts on a set of AR-glasses. Small red dots blink on the side of the black device. Enyd turns to Nurse Saarinen. "If she already has a chip that'll connect her with the augmented reality, why the glasses?"

Nurse Saarinen sets the cup and the straw on a metal tray by the hospital bed or operating table Enyd lies on. "We thought it would be better this way. The glasses make it easier not to get lost between the two realities."

Enyd has no idea what that means.

The doctor takes off the glasses and turns back to face Enyd. "Okay, dear. We'll need to move you back to the penitentiary. You can get back to work. Live your life as usual, though you're not to leave the prison premises at any time. Only a few places in London remain free of the virus. Your place of work is one of them, but I can't promise you your home is. Not anymore."

"And when will I get to travel? Can Samuel get his chip in prison? I don't think he's allowed to leave. Not for a non-mandatory medical procedure."

Nurse Saarinen and Doctor Solomon exchange looks. The nurse turns to check on another patient, and the doctor sits down with Enyd. The hospital bed creaks slightly under her weight.

"Sweetheart. Prisoners are not eligible for the Happiness-Program. Only a few people in London are. Warden Bailey signed a reference letter for you. Only a dozen other government employees have been Chipped and moved to the City of Finland."

"Last I checked, Finland was a country. Not a city."

The doctor's laughter is genuine. Amused. "Well, you must have been under anesthesia longer than we thought." The doctor squeezes her hand tighter when she sees Enyd's horrified expression. "I'm kidding, Enyd. You are perfectly fine. We just need to figure out why your brain is rejecting the chip. Or better yet, why it's stopping it from working."

"And how long will that take?"

The doctor pats Enyd's hand twice, lets go, and takes a step back. "We have our best people working on it. It could be a matter of days, or even hours, until your chip gets the boost it needs. And as soon as it does, we'll send a plane for you."

Enyd forces herself to sit up on the hospital bed. The room spins, and her stomach flips threateningly. "You don't know what's wrong with me. You don't know how to fix this."

"Not at the moment, no. But I will. We will. The good news is that you're not the only one."

"Only one... Only one, what?"

"The only Unchipped person in the City of England."

It's time for lockdown. Enyd waits until the guards get the restless inmates into their cells, knowing that one will remain unlocked. Ever since things started to get really bad outside, the guards have left Samuel's cell unlocked at all times. The prisoners listen to him, more than they listen to the prison staff. Enyd knows it's only a matter of time before the riot will begin. She was surprised when it didn't start a few months ago when the running water was cut off, leaving the prison at the mercy of the old well outside. They've all followed the news closely. Everyone knows what's to come. Soon, not even the uncanny magic in Samuel's soothing words will keep the men from panicking.

As she walks down from the office room upstairs, a group of five prisoners gestures for her to come to their cells. Enyd steps onto the metal ramp above the stairs.

"What's going on, Enyd? We haven't had a single meal today. The kitchen's been closed since last night's lockdown."

She turns around, deciding it'd be better to not start this conversation.

"Yeah, what the bloody hell? And why is part of your hair shaved off?"

More inmates gather in front of their cell doors. Jaxon, the one who speaks for the other hungry men, waves his hand and says, "I know we're all as good as dead, but there are better ways to go than starvation."

Sighing, she turns back around to face them. Enyd swallows and pats her sides. She takes out a USB drive and shoves it into an electrical tablet by the stairs. A metal door rattles open. She makes her way downstairs, doesn't stop by the cells. As she walks to the door that leads into the main hallway, she takes out a keycard that will open another thick metal door. It slides open. Then she heads back upstairs, locks herself in before she buzzes the cell doors open. The guards won't forgive her for this, she knows. But Jaxon is right; doomed or not, these men need to eat.

Jaxon walks up to the open door, and the rest follow. Enyd points at the keycard, resting above the door's electrical lock. "That'll get you into the kitchen. Can you cook? I can't promise you the kitchen staff's going to help you."

"Pff..." Jaxon huffs. "Can I cook..." He waves Enyd off and gestures for his men to follow him. All the men disappear into the hallway. The door remains open. From above, Enyd looks around the room; there should be more than a hundred inmates rushing through their cell doors. Only ten more men hover around the living area.

"You hungry or what? If I were you, I'd not touch a thing Jaxon takes out of the oven. Let alone eat it. But I'm sure you can all find something digestible."

The ten men follow in the footsteps of their fellow prisoners, disappearing into the hallway.

Enyd doesn't need to think hard to know where the rest of them must be. She walks to the control panel—unattended now that so many guards have stopped coming in to work—and flicks through the security cameras, then stops once a live feed from the TV room appears. Only half of the people inside have a place to sit. The rest are standing by the rows of plastic chairs, their arms crossed on their chests.

She presses the audio icon. The news is on. Everyone's quiet. The room's too eerie and static, much too calm for what's airing.

On the TV screen, a row of houses burns. It's somewhere in the suburbs. Then the main street appears on the screen. A man dressed in a jogging suit and a pair of rubber boots stares at the flames. He's holding a young child in his arms. The girl sits and holds onto a red-haired doll pressed against her ash-smudged winter coat. When the camera zooms in on her pouting, serious face, she lifts her hand to wave at it.

People sit doubled over, crying next to their suitcases, backpacks, and duffel bags. Cars are honking, trying to get through the clutter of random obstacles on the road. When a woman stops and coughs into her closed fist, people back away in horror.

But where are they to go? There are only a few facilities in the United Kingdom that this sickness hasn't reached. This prison is one of them. So is a part of the hospital, that now serves as the Chip-Center. Where Enyd was diagnosed as *Unchipped* and sent back to work like nothing had happened.

The pouting girl drops her doll and starts crying. Enyd clears her throat. "The kitchen is now open, my good people. Thought I'd let you know." A few of the inmates standing nearby the speaker turn around to look at it. Rory Mitchell nods at the TV and says, "Shit's crazy, Enyd. What the hell are we supposed to do?"

"You can start by fixing your own damn supper. None of the food deliveries have arrived this week, so you'll need to get by with what we got."

This gets the attention of half the room. The prisoners turn to stare at the speaker.

A riot. It's now or never. And Enyd won't stand a chance.

Enyd continues, "Any trouble or fighting, I'm

sending in the guards. And they are pissed off, more than usual. If Jaxon locked the kitchen door and tries to start some sort of a black market in there, tell him to cut that shit out. Okay?"

Rory leaves the room. One by one, the famished inmates follow him out of the TV room. Only one man remains.

Enyd makes her way downstairs and into the TV room. This time she sits down without waiting for an invitation.

"You're not hungry?"

He sets the white-covered Bible on the empty chair to his left, then reaches for Enyd's hand. Without answering her question or moving his gaze away from the television, his fingers slowly caress the back of Enyd's palm.

"Samuel, you need to eat."

He turns his face to look at her. A half-smile lingers on his dark, handsome face, somehow rough and soft at the same time. This time Enyd doesn't stop herself from running her finger down his bearded cheek. Samuel closes his eyes. His smile deepens.

People screaming and crying—the sound of the news—fades away from around them. Samuel folds his fingers between Enyd's and brings her hand to rest against his broad chest. The only sound in Enyd's ears is the rushing of her blood.

When Samuel reaches for the shaved spot on Enyd's head, she lowers her chin and leans forward. Her forehead rests against Samuel's shoulder. She doesn't care about who might walk in, doesn't care about the consequences. The connection, his touch, fills Enyd with something she can hardly remember ever feeling before. A longing she had long ago abandoned and locked away, labeled too dangerous and risky.

But Samuel is worth the risk. Safe. He's a man of God.

Enyd winces as Samuel's fingers touch the wound the chipping has left on her head. The man pulls back and grabs her by the shoulders. "Enyd, I'm sorry. Curiosity spawns from a lack of knowledge."

"It's okay. I'm fine. Just a complication with the procedure. I'll need to wait here for a while. For them to fix what's broken."

Enyd wishes that Samuel wouldn't ask about it. She has no answers, and the questions burn in her mind like the wound the doctor's drill made early in the morning.

"Do you think less of me now?" Enyd asks him.

"I couldn't. Even if I wanted to."

Samuel pulls her closer, presses Enyd's head against his chest. The sound of his heart beating soothes Enyd into thinking it'll all be okay. Somehow. Someday soon. Though the nagging sound at the back of her skull tells her otherwise.

They sit for a long time. In silence, on the border between sleep and waking. Whenever she's about to drift off, a strange sound reaches her mind.

Intermittent words.

Muffled, like the echo of the ocean.

An accent from a foreign land Enyd's never visited.

Samuel holds her more tightly in his arms. She must have mumbled in her sleep. Something about… regret?

"Don't ask for my forgiveness, Enyd. You're already forgiven, but not by me. Love covers a multitude of sins."

"But Samuel, can't you see? Chipping is our only chance. We must move to the city. Any of them. Then we'll be safe. Looked after. Why is that a sin? Choosing life over death?"

Samuel breathes steadily, his arms still wrapped around her. When the tears start running down her face, she's not sure if they're tears of happiness or sorrow.

"It's the Mark of the Beast, Enyd. No man or a woman of faith would ever accept a microchip. Not without losing their faith. We've talked about this."

They have talked about the Mark. The religious inmates were talking about the Mark of the Beast when the news about the Happiness-Program and chipping first aired about half a year ago. It was supposed to be an option for most of them, living in the United Kingdom. But then, the unknown sickness stopped the hospitals from preparing for the program. Only a handful of people—Enyd included—were chosen to visit the restricted hospital area when Doctor Solomon's team visited from Finland.

"So I can't be a woman of faith now? Not even if my chip doesn't work?"

"I'm not the one to answer that question, Enyd. We all seek for our own truth and choices. And that's okay."

"And what is yours?" Enyd pulls back from Samuel's embrace. She gestures toward the TV. "You can't go out there. Not even if they let me open the prison gates. You'd be dead in a matter of days."

Samuel cups Enyd's face between his rough hands. He leans forward and closes his eyes. When the man kisses Enyd, the tickling sensation in her stomach turns into flames.

Then he kisses her ears. The side of her neck. Her collarbone. In between the kisses, he whispers.

"God is love."

"Whoever lives in love."

"Lives in God."

"And God in them."

The sound of the AR-glasses vibrating against the desk startles Enyd awake. After eating a box of Twinkies and a few of the terrible pieces of crispbread the hospital had packed for her, she must have fallen asleep.

She stands up and stretches her stiff body. Careful not to touch the wound at the back of her head, she fixes her hair, tucking the locks behind her ear. Her leg nudges the office chair. It rolls away from her on the slightly tilted floor and then bangs against a computer stand across the room. Screen savers and blank monitors fill the room. The guards are too busy downstairs to use them.

"You'll hear from us soon." That's all Doctor Solomon had said when they parted ways. Enyd had been left alone to wait for a black van, holding onto a red fabric bag containing a dozen packages of crispbread and a blinking set of AR-glasses.

And here she is again. In her office. Snoozing and eating junk food. Like nothing has changed. Except that the failing chip in her brain has changed everything for her.

As Enyd's about to put on the glasses, the small neon-red lights on the device zap her painfully. The stabbing, numbing agony travels across her skull. Enyd lets go of the glasses like they are suddenly scorching hot in her hands. The glasses fall on the floor, where they keep vibrating. Piercing pain oozes around the puncture wound at the back of her skull.

"Motherf…"

She stares at the device in shock. Suddenly, the intermittent words she's heard inside her head for days become clear. The man's words mix with Enyd's shock of sudden pain.

"Mark of the Beast. Could it be? That's what you're thinking, right? That maybe Samuel was right after all?"

But there's no one in the room. Just like she has been for the past few days, she's all alone. Is this cabin fever?

Enyd holds on to her head and starts pacing around the room. The see-through walls mean that the inmates downstairs can see her meltdown, but she can't calm herself down. What's happening to her? Is she—

"You are not going insane. Unless I have lost it as well. Which is always a likely possibility. Maybe we—"

She bangs her fists repeatedly against her temples. "Who is this? Why are you inside my head?" Then she stops to stare out into space. "Are you—"

A rumbling laugh echoes inside her skull. *"Am I God? Sorry, Enyd. You aren't that lucky. People call me Reverend Marić."*

"I don't understand. Did you attack me through the glasses?"

More echoing laughter. *"Like a genie from a bottle? Again, you're not that lucky."*

"What, then? What the hell is going on?"

She can almost hear the man—this being—shrug his shoulders. *"Honestly? I have no idea. I'm just as surprised as you are. But since the day of my chipping, I've seen you. Heard your voice. Your thoughts. I've felt your fatigue and worry. Whenever it gets too overwhelming, I can block you out. It seems this connection can be controlled by our will."*

"You're definitely a looney. None of this makes any sense."

But doesn't that make her the crazy one?

"Just try this. Close your eyes. Really focus on my voice. Like it's your own voice, your own thoughts. Now, look around. What do you see?"

Enyd holds her breath, her stomach churning. Could she vomit this voice out of her head? Could she dig for the chip, remove it with her stubby fingers, and switch her brain back to whatever normal state it has enjoyed for the last sixty years?

"Just try it. You can come unglued later."

Enyd stares at the screen saver at the other end of the room. Rainbow bubbles bounce against one another, changing direction, only to return again.

"Try it. If you can't see it, I promise you will never hear my voice again."

Shaking her head, Enyd closes her eyes. She turns her focus inward to the place where the thick Slavic accent booms. She imagines it's her own voice. Her own mind.

She sees a waterfront.

A cluttered, partly collapsed harbor.

The tip of a church—a thing from the past.

A square-shaped building, glowing bright neon-purple light. The narrow waterfront reflects that light, creating a mirror illusion. A small, serene port sleeps in the midday sun. "Where…"

"Belgrade, Serbia. Or I guess I should say, City of Serbia."

"Why should you say that?"

A vibrating sound startles Enyd. The AR-glasses rattle steadily against the floor. Like it's a hissing snake about to attack her, Enyd takes a step back.

"You better answer that. They've been buzzing you for quite some time. Just be warned, the glasses will cause you some discomfort. But you must answer anyway."

Enyd keeps staring at the glasses, reluctant to touch them again. "And just ignore the pain?"

"You'll get used to it. As unlikely as it seems."

Slowly, Enyd kneels down and picks up the glasses. Biting her lower lip, she does her best to ignore the stabbing pain as she puts the glasses on.

A trailer of red glowing lights.

Beaming, cheerful people.

Pills of all different shapes, all different colors. It all flashes in front of her eyes. Her stomach flips again.

"Hello? Is this Enyd?" A slightly nasal voice Enyd distantly recognizes speaks through the invisible microphone.

"This is she," Enyd says, her voice raspy and weak.

"Okay, great. Let me turn on the camera."

Enyd sees a woman sitting in a hefty, leather-lined gaming chair. A list of food items flashes by as the smiling woman taps the air.

"Just let me finish with this order real quick."

A food service. Doctor Solomon had mentioned that at the hospital before the procedure. That once Enyd had moved into the city, she'd be able to order in anything on the menu. Breakfast, lunch, supper. Just put on the glasses and let us know what you need.

Big red letters appear on the screen.

50 CC - PAID

Enyd holds her breath and closes her eyes. This is all too much. Too much is changing at once. And she's not where she's supposed to be. She's still here, in the deadly city, trapped in a prison with a hundred doomed inmates and not enough guards to control them.

Samuel's face flashes in front of her eyes. His big hand, resting on a white-covered Bible. On Enyd's thigh. At the back of her neck. Is this the Mark of the Beast?

"Okay, that's all set. So, Enyd? How are you feeling? My name is Nurse Saarinen, in case you don't remember me from the other day."

Enyd opens her eyes. A stern, pale face stares back at her. Nurse Saarinen is smiling, but the smile doesn't reach her eyes. Her high forehead and pointy nose make her look almost robotic.

"Honestly, I'm not feeling so well. I think I've changed my mind, Nurse Saarinen."

"Changed your mind about what?"

"About the chip. I thought I would be moved to the city immediately. That I'd already be a part of the Happiness-Program. But instead, I'm back here. Stuck."

"Where else would you rather be? When we left City of England, most of the people there were dead. I'm quite sure things haven't improved since then."

"Send a plane for me. There are other cities."

Nurse Saarinen sighs on the other end of the line. "Negative. Too risky. The City of England is a hazard zone."

"Then fix it."

"Impossible. The plague mutates quickly and is therefore medication resistant."

"You can't keep me locked in forever."

Enyd can almost hear Nurse Saarinen's indifferent shrug.

"It's your life. Or should I say death? But if you'd

like to prolong one or the other, there is a place where we could transfer you. It's a residential children's home. Kinship Care. Just outside of London. The place is a part of a program called Chip-Charity. A man called Dragan Marić runs the program and needs people like you to participate."

Enyd recognizes the name; the reverend.

"Another Unchipped woman, Margaret, is already there. Too bad, we could have used her talent in the City of Finland. She's a hell of a programmer. But the kids were apparently left alone after the workers fled, so she was needed there."

"Where did they go?"

"Sorry?"

"The workers. Why did they leave the kids alone?"

This time Enyd hears Nurse Saarinen's lab coat rustle as she shrugs. "Beats me. Why does anyone do anything when they're about to die?"

Her apathy gives Enyd the chills.

When Enyd doesn't reply, Nurse Saarinen continues. "We'll send a local helicopter for you. They'll transfer you to Kinship Care first thing tomorrow morning. Bring the AR-glasses. We'll talk later."

Enyd looks over her shoulder. Down in the living quarters, only Jaxon's crew sits around a round table, playing cards. The rest of the prisoners are either in the TV room or burning things in the kitchen's industrial oven. It's just a matter of time before things will turn into chaos. And then, even Samuel won't be able to help her. She has to accept this offer. She has no other choice.

"What about the prison? The inmates? I can't just let them die."

"So, what would you suggest? Should we move a hundred grown men, some sex offenders for sure, to a children's home?"

"These people are good men who made a bad decision once. Surely you know what that's like?"

"Of course! I've made tons of mistakes in my life. But moving a hundred inmates to live in a house full of children won't be one of them."

She clicks her tongue and ends her rant. Nurse Saarinen is clearly done with this debate. Done with this AR-call—done with Enyd. "Just be ready at 8 a.m.; there'll be a car there to take you to the helicopter."

"And the prisoners?"

"What about them?"

"What do I tell them?"

"Oh, I don't know. Just leave the gates open as you go. I'm sure they'll run for the hills. We'll let Mother Nature take care of her own."

The next morning Enyd stands by the front gates, holding a keychain of USB drives and one keycard. The guards have already been picked up, transferred to their new lives, which Enyd knows nothing about. She's the only one left—Enyd and the inmates. The sound of the gates opening will undoubtedly wake up the prisoners if they aren't up already. It's seven-thirty in the morning. She hasn't had a minute of sleep.

A red fabric bag, with the prison's logo printed on its side, hangs from her shoulder. She doesn't have much to take with her. And the driver that Doctor Solomon's crew sent for her won't be making any detours. But it's not the lack of clothing and other belongings that makes Enyd hesitant to leave.

She pushes the USB drive into an electric pad on the side of the prison gate. The thick metal doors slide slowly aside. Once they're wide open, the doors stop moving with a loud *clank*.

Enyd closes her eyes. Now, all she can do is wait.

After a few minutes, distant yells echo across the yard. It's her name they're calling out in wonder and awe. Or is it panic and despair?

The sound of her breath mixes with the thumping of running feet. Enyd is not sure what she wants to happen. The car should be here in thirty minutes. Will the prisoners let her leave? Or will they drag her back inside and hold her hostage?

Will they kill her?

She hears the sound of hurried feet, but they stop just behind her back. Enyd doesn't turn around. She's too ashamed, too beaten to confess the sin she's about to commit. Scared for her life, she's almost certain she'll end up dead. Right here, right now.

But even more than death, she's afraid to see *his* face. Judging her. Hating her.

Jaxon sounds slightly out of breath. "What's going on, Enyd? You left all the doors open."

"I did."

"Are you leaving the front gate open as well?"

"I am."

Surprise fills Jaxon's voice. "Damn."

Jaxon peeks over his shoulder, silencing the ripple of mumbles and chattering behind him. Once it's silent again, he gazes upon the green hills that roll out in front of the gate. In the distance, the city glows a strange, red light. Is the city on fire? Or is it the tiles they've installed all around, before the plague took the city?

"You going there? To the city?" Jaxon asks, nodding toward the red light. Enyd sighs and lowers her chin. Jaxon takes it as an answer, yes or no, Enyd doesn't know. "Maybe we're immune to that shit."

"And what shit is that?"

"The shit that kills everybody."

"Maybe."

Jaxon moves his weight from one foot to another. His twitching hands and restless feet scream of his urge to run for the hills. His reflex to make a run for newfound freedom. One of the inmates clears his throat behind them. "We going or staying or what?"

A grin spreads across Jaxon's face. His eyes reflect his hunger for a new beginning, his willingness to leave this place behind. "Fuck it. What's the worst thing that could happen? We can either die of hunger here or live a little. I'd rather hit a few pubs and drink whatever whiskey's left before I cash in my chips."

Enyd wonders if the pun is intended. But the man doesn't have a chip. None of them do. They have never made the cut.

The five men start walking toward the red glow in the distance. A man walks over to her, stands so close that Enyd's shoulder brushes against his bicep. His folded hands hold a white-covered bible and a set of rosary prayer beads.

They watch the five men walk across the field. Once they reach the green hills, Enyd holds her breath but forces herself to watch what happens next.

But nothing happens.

Just a red glow, an illusion, a reflection that swallows Jaxon and his crew into the city.

And just like that, they're gone.

More footsteps reach the standing couple. Without a word, one by one, the men make their way out of the prison gates, onto the field, up the rolling hills, and into the red light. Not one of them collapses on the ground to gasp for air. But it's just a matter of weeks, maybe days.

It seems like hours. They stand, Enyd and Samuel, and watch as the inmates disappear into the red light. At some point, Samuel reaches for Enyd's hand. The prayer beads press against her palm. She welcomes this slightly painful sensation, the only thing grounding her in this moment. Everything else is too surreal.

Suddenly there are no more silhouettes to follow.

Not a single person remains on the horizon. But they keep on standing. Hand in hand. Watching. Listening. Waxwings fly above the prison gates. Enyd looks up and hopes that the birds will land somewhere nearby. Maybe she'll see a sign of the plague... a rotting wing, or a featherless head. The news said nothing about the animals. The screen was only filled with bruised, decaying people.

The black van appears out of nowhere. It parks fifteen feet away from the prison's front gate. The driver remains seated inside the vehicle; nobody steps out. The motor's steady purr sounds patient and demanding at the same time. Is it too late for her to change her mind? Did she ever even have the privilege of choice?

Enyd holds Samuel's hand tighter. The beads press against her palm like rusty nails. "You could come with me. I can talk to them. Make them see..." Her words trail away as Samuel turns to look at her. His big, rough hands cup her face. The kiss is different from last time. Hopeless yet hopeful. The first and the last of its kind.

When Samuel says nothing after their long kiss, Enyd continues her pointless rant. "Maybe the plague is false news. Maybe all of it is. Just the government trying to scare us into staying where we are. For everyone to get chipped, so we're all part of an easily controlled system. Maybe it *is* the Mark of the Beast."

Samuel smiles. His rough thumbs caress Enyd's blushing cheeks. Even in the middle of the silent chaos, when there's no more threat of getting caught, she still feels overwhelmed by the bundle of feelings that Samuel arouses in her.

"Professing to be wise, they became fools." Samuel moves his hands to hold Enyd by her shoulders. His Bible presses softly against Enyd's neck. "But there *is* a plague, Enyd. This is the end. They have a few days, maybe only hours until their time on this earth—in this reality—comes to an end. And it's okay. If we live, we live for the Lord. And if we die, we die for the Lord. So, whether we live or die, we belong to the Lord."

He places the Bible and the beads into Enyd's hands and kisses her forehead. "I hope that one day you will do His work. Help others see what I see and help them see the sign. Help them feel Him. When you feel as if you've lost yourself—that's when you'll find Him. That's my last wish. To you."

Then, Samuel starts walking.

Enyd opens her mouth, but she's become mute. She listens for the birds, for words, for any sign of life. But she's become deaf. She wants to run after Samuel, grab him by the back of his overalls, force him to return. But she's lost all control over her limbs.

All she can do is watch. Watch Samuel follow the steps of the other inmates.

Into the field.

Up the rolling hills.

Into the red glow.

CHAPTER 4
IN THE BLIMP'S SHADE

The raindrops fall on Enyd's bare arms and calves. Their piercing coldness feels like a thousand broken prayer beads, plummeting from the sky to punish her sinful skin.

She should dance in the rain. Move her hips to the tune the reverend inside her head is humming. Ignore the agony in her ankles. Forget the images of two beaten girls, counting to a hundred. Their body and spirit torn into hundreds of little beads.

But her body is made of lead. Her mind is blank, save for Samuel's words repeating in her ears: "When you feel as if you've lost yourself—that's when you'll find Him." He's been right, all along. God is the answer. She needs to do everything as Samuel once told her.

"You should celebrate!" Nurse Saarinen had said. But Marić had another kind of message. "Enyd, I don't know what happened in the basement, but it has clearly upset you very much. Maybe we should—" This is where Enyd had cut the connection. What's about to happen next has nothing to do with the reverend.

One million and twenty thousand chip credits. Overflowing praise for their latest warning video. A victory for the Happiness-Program. Perfect injuries! Outstanding resemblance to the real plague! Relatable agony and distress. "I bet the city gates will stay clear tonight. I bet none of the Chipped will want to share the poor girls' fate."

That's one thing Nurse Saarinen got right: poor girls. But it's never what Nurse Saarinen says, it's how she says it. With glee. Excitement and satisfaction.

Enyd had left the girls in the basement and told the boys to clean up and lock the door. Back upstairs, she sent the video in and listened to Nurse Saarinen's excited rant about it through the AR-set. Then she tossed the phone and the AR-set back in the drawer, walked out of the office, out of the library, and into the yard. Here, she's been standing in the rain for a small eternity. Blending in with the dead grass and mud puddles.

A dark blanket of storm clouds turns the dusk into night. She should be cold in her thin white gown, but Enyd doesn't focus on such meaningless things: cold, discomfort, hunger. It makes no difference to her now. All she needs is a sign.

She feels the reverend with her at the back of her mind. The Serbian man is intelligent. He can read the room—or a mind—from two thousand miles away. He can read Enyd like an open Bible.

The images of bruised, swollen limbs gnaw a hole in her chest. Small relentless teeth chew and nibble on her until her whole body is filled with burrowing rodents. But instead of worms, the tunnels are filled with something more dreadful: Violence. Sin. Regret.

Her throat feels swollen. Breathing is hard. Too hard, like the devil himself sits on her broad, curvy chest, holding on to her neck with two flaming hands.

The yard around her spins. Like a small girl stuck on a carousel that is spinning around too fast, she begs for it to end. She prays without knowing how. For all of this to go away. For the Beast to leave her be.

Enyd falls to her knees. Mud splashes around her, staining her white gown. She sinks her hands into the dirt, her knees sinking deeper into the wet ground.

"Be merciful to me, oh God. Wash away my sins. Wash away all my evil. Make me clean from my sin."

They are Samuel's words. No—the reverend's words. Or are they her own?

The rain gets heavier. Images of Ava's swollen face won't leave her be. Neither will those of Hannah, curled into a sobbing ball in the red corner of the basement room. Blood dripping off the old wooden chair. The boys, taking off their leather gloves, stashing away their rolling pins.

Until next time.

Enyd wails at the images. Screams at the AR-cameras. The videos. All the blackened fingers and broken bones.

"What to do? What to do? What to do?"

Ignoring the wet mud smudged across her face, Enyd wipes her nose with the back of her hand.

"I have to kill the Beast. Save them from the Beast. Samuel, just give me a sign…"

The pressure grows at the back of her head. Margaret taps her. She's been tapping her for a while. But Enyd keeps blocking the connection.

So crowded… in her head. So much noise. So much sin. Too much Beast. Too little Samuel.

The pressure grows more demanding. Two people. Both tapping her at the same time. Would they be able to hear each other? Margaret and the reverend? How does this madness work? Does it even matter?

With a long exhale, she lets go. The connection opens. Meaningless, empty words take over. Two voices mixing with each other.

"Enyd, whatever it is you did, you only did it because you had to blah blah. If the Chipped don't get their blah blah blah. They'd stop sending you blah." It's the reverend's voice.

Meaningless. Emptiness.

"Come back. Blah. We can blah blah. Blah." Margaret. Pleading, foolish Margaret.

What do they know? They're never there when the rolling pins come out. They just check in to judge her, to argue, or to check the score on the bulletin board.

She presses her forehead into the wet ground and weeps. "Just one sign… any sign… Show me how… *Guide* me…"

But all she sees are the images.

Hannah's belly bump.

Ava's blurred eyes sedated with blockers and pain.

The London Eye—covered with blood, corpses, guts, and limbs. Some of it isn't real. Which part? What is?

"They are sinners. They need to be punished for their sins. Open that Bible of yours, Enyd. Read. Soon you'll see. Everything you do here is for the greater good."

Enyd closes her eyes and imagines the white, plastic-covered Bible. Every scratch, every perfect imperfection carved on its hard cover. Each made by Samuel. His rough but loving hands.

The Bible is grounding. It helps her slow down her breathing. Helps her sit down in the rain.

"I have the chip. I am marked. Doesn't that make me a sinner?"

"And what if it does? And aren't you paying for those sins now? Isn't this your absolution?"

Somewhere across the yard, someone yells her name. A young man. Not Samuel. Samuel is in paradise. He earned his place in forever after as he died from the plague. A good man. God's gift.

A long scratch on the back of the white-covered Bible. The smooth surface of each prayer bead. A rough but gentle hand. A reassuring smile. Samuel was right. How can he not have been? About everything.

"Samuel. A sign… please."

She pushes her weight up and off the ground.

Standing up, she can feel the phantom pain of Samuel's prayer beads against the palms of her hands. She presses her hands into fists, just as she's seen Ava do a hundred times. "In him, we have redemption through his blood."

"That's more like it. You're only doing God's work. The sacrifices we make are for all of us. For our place in eternity. We must earn it. They must earn it. With chip credit."

Like Samuel did. Like he would if he were still here. But he's not. It's just Enyd and the sinners. A deaf woman with two endlessly hungry young men who have grown to enjoy violence. Ava. Hannah and Noah. *The baby.*

She blinks rapidly. That's it. A sign. The sign.
Baby Samuel.

Enyd ignores the aching of her ankles. Ignores the children staring at her as she makes her way through the backdoor and the downstairs hallway. Her mud-soaked gown leaves a wet trail on the wall-to-wall carpet.

Curious heads peek out of bedroom doors. "Why are you still up? It's bedtime, go, go, go!" she yells. She doesn't turn around to see whether they are obeying her orders or not. They would. They will.

Enyd makes her way to the library and shuts the door. She walks across the room, pushes the office door open, and closes it behind her. She can barely hear the sound of the rusty lock clicking from all the blood and adrenaline rushing in her ears.

A steady, nagging pain starts from the back of her head. It could be Margaret tapping her; it could be the reverend. It could be that antichrist, Kaarina. The one who walks through the valley of death without collapsing. Her pale skin had been bruise-free. Her steps steady and strong. Only a thing of true malevolence could survive the plague.

But Enyd will burn this place down before she'll let the she-devil walk through Kinship Care's front gate.

She unlocks the drawer and pulls out the AR-glasses. It's almost ten p.m., but Nurse Saarinen will answer Enyd's call. She carries her AR-set everywhere. Like the pathetic, controlled sheep she is, Nurse Saarinen lives inside that devilish thing. Worships the Beast.

This time, the sharp pain at Enyd's temples hardly makes her wince. Shaking—out of rage, not fear—she stares at the neon-red trailer, flashing in front of her eyes.

"Arnie, call Nurse Saarinen. City of Finland."

CALL INITIATED

She'll show them all. Punish them. She'll make them suffer. For the greater good.

Three white dots appear on the screen. While Enyd waits for Nurse Saarinen to pick up, she stares at an advertisement. A pill to soothe minds and relax bodies. Accessible to anyone living in the city. VIP pill for VIP people. More sin for the sinners.

The three dots vanish against the neon-red background. Nurse Saarinen doesn't turn on the camera, but her voice booms in Enyd's ears. "Enyd? Is everything alright? It's awfully late." Nurse Saarinen sounds more baffled than irritated by the unscheduled call.

"Everyone who does evil hates the light and will not come into the light for fear that their deeds will be exposed."

The line goes mute. Finally, Nurse Saarinen says, "I don't do riddles, Enyd. What is it you need? All calls should be—"

"It's not a riddle. You and everything you stand for are evil. You practice ungodliness and spread error concerning the Lord—"

"Enyd, that's enough. Let's end this before you say something we'll both regret. The video is already streaming. The airship is on its way to you. It'll arrive first thing tomorrow morning. Just be ready with the laser around 8 o'clock. Now go to bed, okay?"

Enyd's voice rises. "The hungry they leave empty, and from the thirsty, they withhold water."

"Have you lost your mind? Enyd, you have over a hundred children to take care of. Get ahold of yourself."

Enyd gasps for air. She stands up, makes a cross on her chest. With her voice steady, she says, "Jesus did not eat anything for forty days and forty nights. At the end of that time, he was hungry."

"At the end of that time, he would be dead. Enyd, may I speak with Margaret? Is she there with you?"

Enyd reaches for the glasses and pulls them away from her face, just enough for her to see the AR-camera blinking in the corner of the room. She breathes steadily, self-assured and at peace. Then she says, "We won't be sending you any more videos. We don't need your charity either. Do not send us any more food."

"That's just absurd, let me talk with—"

The AR-glasses fall onto the floor. Enyd's rubber-soled slippers hover above them. She steps on the glasses, stomping, breaking—trying to crush them into little black pieces. When the glasses are twisted up beyond repair, Enyd hurls them against the wall and stomps out of the room.

The airship looks like a small cloud up in the distance. The early morning sun beams down through the clouds. The food delivery is on time, just as it always is. Enyd carries a laser pointer and its tripod, rushing to get to the farthest hill on the premises. It's the closest one to the red glowing city and at the opposite side of the yard from where the cargo usually lands.

Too focused on working the tripod, she doesn't stop Margaret from entering her mind.

"Enyd. The boys. Are smashing. Arnie. Almost all cameras. Are. Out. What is. Going on?"

Shaking her head, she blocks the connection. Good. The boys should be finished with the last of the cameras any minute now. Arnie has left the building.

Enyd hurries toward the highest point in the yard. She's done this a hundred times, using the old military technology which the cities now use for transporting goods. But never has she aimed the laser anywhere other than Kinship Care's backyard.

The airship is now close enough for Enyd to read the letters painted on its side.

CHIP-CHARITY

Taking stumbling strides, defying the never-ending pain in her achy ankles, she makes her way up the hill. She places the laser target designator down. Once the tripod stands sturdy on the slippery ground, she clicks the device on. Carefully she turns the laser pointer until the red laser beam points outside the fence line. With the CS-key locking them all in, no one will be able to reach it. They will all stay. The higher power will take care of them. Samuel will look after them.

Enyd points the laser further, two green hills down and toward the city.

"Enyd! No!"

It takes her a moment to realize who is yelling at her from the home's back door. The voice is somehow off yet familiar. It must be the first time Enyd has heard Margaret scream out loud.

Enyd moves her focus from the woman—running and slipping on the puddles left behind by yesterday's rain—to look at the airship. "Come on, come on..." Almost there. Behind her back, she hears Margaret slip and land on the ground. It takes her a moment to get back to her feet. That has bought the ship some time.

The Beast can keep their cursed goods. God will

provide them with everything they need.

The children will learn.

Enyd will lead them all into salvation. No more co-operating with the devil. They will find their own way.

Catching Enyd by surprise, Margaret pulls her away from the tripod. Enyd slips and lands in the mud, softly enough to not break any bones, but hard enough to feel a nasty twinge in her left hip. Enyd reaches for the tripod on the ground. The red X is nowhere to be seen.

"Have you. Lost. Your. Mind?"

With all the strength she has left, Enyd pushes Margaret aside. Then she crawls forward, toward the fallen tripod. She stumbles to her knees, then moves to stand. Her feet slip on the wet soil, and she falls back down on her backside. Sliding downhill, Enyd watches as Margaret crawls toward the laser pointer, her desperate eyes flickering between the tripod and the approaching blimp. It's very close now. In less than a minute, it will cross the hill Enyd wants the cargo to land on.

Margaret gets to the tripod. She places its legs back into the ground, points the laser into the middle of the yard. This is where the supply has landed for the last two years. "You want. Us to. Starve?" Enyd had no idea the woman could sound this outraged.

Slowly, careful not to startle Margaret and send her running down the hill with the laser, Enyd gets up. She tries to wipe some of the mud off her pants and jacket but ends up smudging it more. "You're right. I'm so sorry, Margaret. What was I thinking?"

The deaf woman's too busy holding onto the tripod and keeping the laser pointed in the middle of the yard to read Enyd's lips. Enyd has to tap her. *I'm so sorry, Margaret. I'm not sure what got into me.* Enyd takes a few steps uphill and toward the woman. *You want me to do it? Sometimes the laser wobbles a bit.*

"I got. This."

Her back to Enyd, Margaret stares through the lens, doing her best to keep the tripod in place. Enyd takes another step closer. Then another. *You need to tilt it a bit better. If the X is not centered, it may not take.* Enyd looks up. The blimp is now traveling across the hill where she meant the cargo to land. *Do you need help?*

"It is. Centered. We're fine."

Just as Margaret looks away from the lens and up to the sky, Enyd launches herself at her. This time the tripod stays upright. Only the two women land on the wet ground. With two hands, Enyd pushes Margaret down the slippery hill. She rolls down the hill like a dreidel, trying to grab onto something to break her fall. A surge of adrenaline helps Enyd scramble up from the ground.

Enyd tilts the laser pointer back up and aims at the hill the airship's hovering over. The blimp's sensors hit the X. The cargo bay doors open, releasing dozens of drones to deliver white plastic boxes of all sizes. One by one, the goods glide through the air and fall neatly on the hillside. Another successful food delivery from the City of Finland.

Only this time, it's not going to end up in the kitchen pantry.

As the blimp throws its shade across the yard, Margaret climbs up the hill. She stands next to Enyd, staring at a month's worth of food, medicine, and supplies in the distance.

"I do not. Understand."

Enyd turns to Margaret so she can read her lips. "One does not live by bread alone, but by every word that comes forth from the mouth of God."

"They're children. They need food."

"It's the Beast. Satan's work. It has been all along. The Lord, your God, shall you worship and Him alone shall you serve."

"Why are you. Talking like. That. All the. Cameras. Are destroyed."

Enyd's eyes drill into Margaret. "Are you questioning my words, Sister? Because he speaks through me. Is it your intention to keep his commandments?"

"He would not. Let us. Starve. Enyd, this is. Getting way out. Of hand."

Margaret turns to leave. Her steps create distance between Enyd and her.

It starts to rain again. Enyd looks up to the sky, looks for the airship, but can't see a glimpse of it. Out in the distance, the white boxes lie in a neat circle. One of the boxes has landed wrong. It lies on its side, its lid cracked open, but Enyd's too far away to see what's inside.

She hears the back door shut with a bang. Margaret

will come around. She always does. She's too weak to rise against Enyd. Too weak to do anything without her. Just like the rest of them. The boys will protest, of course. They love their food, even the crappy crispbread and the bland porridge they spoon up every morning. But they will learn to be humble. They'll learn to control their urges, their filthy desires. Just like the boy whose sweater Hannah wears down in the basement. Enyd doesn't need proof. God sees, and she will do his dirty work. They will all feel the consequences of breaking the rules under Enyd's and Samuel's roof.

No more sinning.

Enyd picks up the tripod. She folds the legs and tucks the target designator under her arm. With careful steps, she follows Margaret. The wind tosses raindrops into her face, but she barely notices. It's finally here. Her calling. Samuel's last wish.

A half-smile lingers on Enyd's lips as she walks through the rain and wind. A new-found strength in her step and the tripod swinging under her arm, she marches back to the house. At the back door, she stops to listen. It's quiet. Like the whole world is waiting for her next move. For Samuel's move. God's.

With one strong pull, she opens the partly jammed door and steps inside. In the distance, she hears hurried footsteps, hustle, chaos. But she's not worried or rushed. She has the rest of her life to put things in order. She's now in full control. As she should have always been.

She sets the tripod by the doorway. Tapping for

Margaret, a calm, soothing sensation takes over her body. When the words echo through her mind, she's not sure if they are hers or whether they belong to the reverend, Samuel, or God himself.

"For those whom the Lord loves, he disciplines. And He scourges every son whom He receives."

The soles of her rubber slippers squeak as Enyd makes her way up the stairs. It's quiet. Too quiet for it to be noon in Kinship Care, home to more than a hundred people.

"Oliver? Thomas?" Her call sends little footsteps running away behind the closed doors. Why would the children hide from Enyd? Can't they see they are finally free?

Enyd needs to find the boy. Noah. She needs to show him what he's done.

A door opens to her right. A small, round face peeks out. Owena blinks rapidly, staring at Enyd. She stops by the little girl, kneels down to talk to her. "Owena, be a good girl and point me to Noah's bedroom." She should remember, but it's usually Margaret, Oliver, or Thomas who deals with the teenage boys.

Owena tilts her head from side to side. Her wide eyes never leave Enyd as she contemplates her request. "Why? Is Noah in trouble? I like Noah. I don't want anything bad to happen to him. Did he steal bad things, Sister Enyd? Are you going to send him to hell?"

It's Enyd's turn to cock her head in wonder. "Bad things?"

The girl nods slowly. "Did Noah steal a machine that controls minds? Like Ava did?"

Just as Enyd's about to answer, another door opens down the hallway. Thomas quietly orders someone to stay inside. Carefully, he slips through the doorway and shuts the bedroom door behind him. He turns and freezes as his eyes fall on Enyd.

"Is Noah in there?" she asks, tempted to kneel over and rub her aching ankles.

"Nope. Not here. Enyd, what's going on? Margaret is freaking out. She told all the kids to stay in their bedrooms. It's almost time for afternoon tea and biscuits. I get why you wanted to destroy the cameras. It was about time. But why is everyone hiding?"

"There'll be no biscuits today, Thomas. Where is Noah?"

Thomas looks at the door next to him. Two long strides and Enyd's opened the door. Inside, three boys sit on their bunk beds, all looking at Enyd as if she's suddenly grown horns. She recognizes his roommates. "Where's Noah, boys? I'm not going to ask twice."

Footsteps echo from the stairway. Oliver walks in, spreading his hands. "Care to tell me what's gotten into Margaret? She's taken Noah and locked herself in the basement room. Most of the food's gone from the kitchen. Even the crispbread."

Thomas scoffs and turns to look at Oliver. "Who

cares if the old hag took the rest of that cardboard you call bread? Don't you know what day today is?"

"The day you finally put a sock in it?"

"It's delivery day, you wanker—"

Enyd lifts her hand, and the room falls silent. The boys on their bunkbeds exchange a look. Enyd narrows her eyes and looks around the room.

"They're all in the basement?"

Thomas taps his feet against the floor. Nobody says anything. Enyd folds her hands behind her back and walks over. His foot stops tapping and freezes on the spot. "And why are you here? In Noah's room? Snooping around?"

Oliver cocks his head and looks at them in wonder. "Yeah, why?" When Enyd gives him the side-eye, Oliver backs off. Enyd stares Thomas down. "Well?"

The boy is shaking slightly. He's holding onto something red, behind his back. A fabric bag. Enyd reaches behind Thomas' back and yanks the bag from him. She rips it open. Socks, underwear, a hoodie, two thin blankets, a travel pillow, and at least a dozen granola bars. The good kind of granola bars. With chocolate.

"Where did you get these?"

The boy shakes his head from side to side. "I'm sorry, Sister Enyd. Margaret told me to get Noah's things. To deliver them down to the basement after nightfall. She said I'd get the granola bars. Something about them being the only food I'd have to eat. I don't know what's going on, but you know how much I love—"

The look on Enyd's face is enough to stop Thomas in the middle of his sentence. *Sister Margaret. You are many things, but a thief?* But the deaf woman doesn't answer her tapping.

Thomas drops the bag on the floor. He backs away to sit on an empty bunkbed. Noah's bed. Enyd picks up the bag. She takes out six of the granola bars and hands them to Oliver. Then, she picks out another six, walks to Thomas, and hands them over.

"You don't work for Margaret," she says. "These bars weren't hers to give. But don't get me wrong. You don't work for me either." Enyd lifts her chin and looks down her nose at Thomas. "Commit your work to the Lord, and your plans will be established." She gestures Oliver and Thomas to come closer. The younger boys in the room stare at them, wide-eyed and confused. It doesn't matter; she only needs Oliver and Thomas. They'll be part of her plan. *His* plan.

"I want you to listen very carefully. Here's what's going to happen next."

Careful not to land on her buttocks again, Enyd takes her time getting down the stairs to the basement. Left foot. Right foot. Left foot. Right foot. One stone step at a time. Her fingers wrap around Samuel's prayer beads inside her pocket. With her free hand, she grabs on to the railing. She finally makes her way down.

The basement reeks of mold, despair, and something foul—a new scent Enyd can't quite put her finger on. Have the boys burned something other than wood to keep the building warm? Old clothing? Bloody towels?

The boys should be done in the attic by now. They should have found what Enyd has sent them for. Now she'll just need to get Margaret to open the basement door. Talking sense to the deaf woman is something Enyd's good at. She's done it before. Maneuvered her mind, bent her will. And she'll do it once again.

Her slippers steady on the concrete floor, Enyd turns toward the basement door. The furnace hums from the other room, warm and inviting. For a moment, Enyd thinks about turning around, laying the blankets in Noah's bag in front of the fire. The adrenaline rush has left her fatigued and weak, but this is not the time to rest. She raps her knuckles against the rough wood.

"Margaret? Ava? Open the door."

Not a peep.

"Noah? I brought your clothes. More blankets. Thomas told me what happened. I'm not angry. I just want to talk."

Something or someone moves against the door. Then silence.

"Ava? Are you okay in there? Did Margaret remember to bring your medicine? I'm worried, my child. Come open the door, and we'll talk this through."

This pleading feels like it's ripping holes in her,

tearing her chest apart. The maddening need for salvation growing inside her is getting impossible to contain. It pushes up through her skin like her blood is suddenly boiling.

His will. His last wish.

Finally: a familiar pressure at the back of her head. Enyd takes a step back, glaring at the door. *Margaret? I need you to let me inside.*

"It's not Margaret. It's me. Ava."

Enyd winces in shock. The blockers. Margaret must have forgotten them. The affect has worn off.

"She didn't forget, you sick fuck. She told me everything. I guess I'm not diabetic after all, am I?"

"Mind your language, child. Diabetic or not, you're still in God's house."

"Fuck your language. Fuck this house. And most of all—fuck you, Enyd. I want my phone. I want to find my mother. And I want to get the fuck out of here."

Boiling blood.

Swarming chest maggots.

A sinner, speaking the words of the devil.

But Enyd is strong. Doing God's work. She'll end this madness. Punish those who spread their filthy sins across this house. Like a plague. *They* are the plague.

Two sets of footsteps echo from the stairway walls. Oliver and Thomas stop behind her, each resting an antique bolt action rifle against his shoulder.

"If I promise you'll get your phone back," Enyd says, "will you open this door?"

Through the open connection, through Ava's eyes, Enyd scans the basement room. Hannah lies in the corner in pain. Her curly brown hair is spread across Noah's lap. Margaret places a wet rag on Hannah's forehead. The yellow-blue bruises around her left arm, the one stretched out to Margaret, hurt Enyd's eyes. But only for a second.

The sinner should have known better.

Ava turns around to face the door again. To face Enyd. "Sure, I'll open the door."

Enyd frowns. She's doubtful but takes a half-step back anyway. The boys murmur something behind her, but they shut up when Enyd shushes them.

"I'll open the door as soon as you admit that you're a sadist and a hypocrite."

Oliver lowers his rifle, sets it against the stone wall. "Do you want me to kick it open?"

Thomas follows his example, ready to take down the heavy door. Enyd looks at the two boys, estimating their strength. A piece of chocolate stains the side of Thomas's upper lip. Oliver cracks his knuckles, ready for action. Could they take the door down? Maybe they could. After years of hard labor, dragging, pulling, lifting, pushing, beating... One door would be nothing.

Enyd steps away from the door and nods at Thomas and Oliver. Together they turn their shoulders toward the heavy door, count to three, and bounce their body weight against the wooden surface. A dull *thump* is all they get.

"Again," Enyd says, tapping for Ava. Then tapping for Margaret. No one answers. She feels another Unchipped connection lingering nearby. There shouldn't be another one. The strange new connection is not inside Kinship Care's walls but somewhere nearby.

The She-Devil and her crew. Kaarina, getting closer. How does she know where they are?

The two boys crash against the wooden door. They take three steps back, to gain momentum. Their bodies slam against the door again, but the door won't budge an inch. A connection to the room opens again. Through Margaret's eyes, Enyd sees Hannah, sipping water to help her swallow two white tablets. Painkillers from Enyd's office drawer. The girl lingers between consciousness and sleep.

"Enyd. You need. To let us. Go. The plague. Is not real. If you let me. I can. Explain—"

Enyd lifts her hand to tell the boys to stop. They're hurting their shoulders, and the door is clearly more heavily built then the two of them put together. Out of breath, they rub their arms and collapse on the floor next to the rifles.

I never said you can't come out. Can't you hear us trying to set you free? It's better to get Hannah upstairs—

"We are. Leaving. Kinship Care. Enyd."

Enyd blinks in surprise. This is not something she's considered. *You'd rather walk into certain death than come out and pay for your sins?*

"Listen to me. The plague. Is not. Real."

The boiling feeling under Enyd's skin returns… if it ever left her. How stupid is this woman? She's always considered Margaret as an equal. Someone intelligent. Sophisticated. Sure, it bothered Enyd that she constantly challenged her leadership. And she's not a true believer. Not like Enyd or Samuel.

Margaret. Be reasonable. I know things are hard to understand right now. But killing the girls is not the answer. Killing yourself is not the answer. Think about the baby. Little Samuel. It's a sign, Sister Margaret. The baby is our savior.

A mocking laughter echoes in Enyd's skull. It's Ava, breaking in on their silent conversation. *"Little Samuel? Enyd, you've lost it. Gone barmy. Positively bonkers. Nutted up,"* Ava says, mockery in her voice. *"Tell Oliver and Thomas to back off with those ancient rifles. Have those things ever even been fired? They'll probably lose half a face and an arm if they use them."*

Staring at Enyd, not knowing about the conversation going on, the boys get up from the floor. Oliver steps closer. His hand hovers above Enyd's shoulder but then drops back down. "Enyd? Should we have another go? I could swear I felt the wood give in the last time we—"

"No."

"But we have to get in—" Thomas' hand on Oliver's shoulder interrupts him in the middle of the sentence. Neither of the boys has ever been good at reading the room, but Thomas has always been a bit more street-smart. He clears his throat to get Enyd's attention. Enyd stares at the closed door, her thoughts bouncing around in her busy mind.

"Enyd. You want us to go?"

"No."

The boys exchange a look. Knowing better than to disobey, they back away and sit on the stone stairs. Enyd's fingertips investigate the dents in the wooden door. Small splinters scratch against her skin, and she lets them sink into her flesh.

"Margaret? Open this cursed door. Please. Let's take Hannah back upstairs. Oliver and Thomas are here to help."

"With. Rifles?"

Enyd ignores Margaret's question and the rage in her voice. She won't budge. Enyd needs to find the weakest link in the room, and it's not Margaret. Ava's too headstrong. Hannah is too pregnant and in shock.

"Noah. This is no way to start your life as a father. What kind of a father puts their baby in this kind of danger? Step forward, good man. Open the door. Help us help you."

A short rustling sound reaches Enyd's ears. Noah has left the hard, red bed in the corner of the room. He's walking to the door, despite someone trying to stop him.

"You think you know everything, don't you?" The thick wood can't muffle the wrath in his voice. "Think again, Enyd. And while you're at it, think really hard about this place you've created. The fairy tales you shove down our throats year after year. Blackmail and violence. Just because we stay quiet doesn't mean we believe any of it."

"Just open this—"

"And you think those who follow you are innocent? Just because they agree to beat us when you tell them to? Just because they only use the phones and tablets when you're not there to see? Eat your junk food and drink your soda?"

Enyd hears Oliver and Thomas freeze on the stairs. They've been stealing from her?

"Don't speak in riddles, Noah." Enyd doesn't let his mocking laughter silence her. "What do you mean?"

"Margaret is right. We can leave this god-forsaken hellhole. There's no such thing as the plague. Kaarina's coming to help us."

It's Enyd's turn to laugh. "And here I thought you didn't believe in fairy tales."

"The plague. Was planted by those. Who created. The Happiness-Program."

"Planted? Why?"

"For the people who. Didn't want to. Join the Chipped. And for those. Who were. Unworthy. Or so. They said."

No. That's not true. It can't be.

"The program created. A weaponized. Version of the Marburg. Virus. When consumed. It acts. As a poison."

She's full of it. Bluffing. Why would they wipe out the

whole city? Why would anyone hurt Samuel willingly?

"It was designed. To be waterborne. The ones who. Were cleared to be chipped. Were moved elsewhere. Until the cleaning operation. Was done."

The hospital.

Nurse Saarinen pouring her another cup of water. Water they had brought in with them. "Remember, no tap water." That's what Doctor Solomon had said.

Could it be?

"Enyd, we can. Get out of here. We can get Hannah. To a hospital. Save the. Baby."

Baby Samuel.

"Get rid of. The rifles. Gather. The children. Save. Yourself, Enyd. I won't. Hold a. Grudge."

Enyd leans her forehead against the door's splintery surface. Head spinning with images and words. Feelings from the past and the present mingle in her mind. Blending, stirring, scrambling. Until it's all an aching bundle of disbelief and boiling anger.

The plague.

Red, glowing lights on the horizon.

Kaarina and her false prophecy.

Samuel's sign.

It's tempting. To believe the plague is just another trick of the devil. But that's what the devil does: tempts you. Lures you. Feeds you lies.

"You're wrong. You made it all up."

"Wake up, Enyd," Noah huffs, rage in his voice. "It's not us who can't see the truth. You think it's me who got Hannah pregnant? Think again. Think really, really hard."

Enyd stays quiet, holds her breath.

"Why don't you ask your precious boys who the father is?"

No. Sweet baby Jesus. No.

Enyd bangs her head against the door. Two sets of footsteps back off inside the room. Oliver and Thomas jump up and hurry to the door. "Enyd, let us help—"

Another bang stops them in their tracks. Enyd lifts the prayer beads and places them against the scar at the back of her skull. She presses the beads against her hair.

Bang.

"Enyd, we really have nothing to do with the—"

Bang.

"Okay, okay. We were just having some fun. It wasn't supposed to end up—"

Bang.

"We didn't know she was old enough to… we thought she'd never…"

Enyd's eyes fly open. Her eyesight blurred, she stares at the carvings in the wooden door. The splinters on them spin around. They whirl and pulse. As the boys' words sink in, her blood boils faster. Harder.

"You… *raped* Hannah?"

Enyd wants to be surprised. Wants to be shocked. But the more she thinks about it, the more she knows it's true. These two spoiled, privileged, chocolate-bar-munching heathens.

135

Oliver shows his palms. "Whoa! Hey! Strong words, Sister Enyd. No one raped anybody. We found a video... *videos*, on the Chip-network one night. It was a stupid idea, I know. We know. But no one had sinned for weeks and weeks. Couple of bruised fingers, no real work. We got bored, is all."

Enyd turns around. She stares at the two boys. Her hand still holds the prayer beads against the slit where the Mark of the Beast once entered her brain. "Punishment is not there for your pleasure. It's a necessary evil," she says, shaking her head slowly. "You got... *bored*? So, you went into my office. Broke into the drawers. Stole a smartphone. Watched porn. And *raped* one of my children? One of *His* children?"

Thomas and Oliver glance at the rifles, resting against the wall. "We didn't think... I mean, she watched it with us... Besides, it's not as bad as the rolling pin. No damage done."

They're possessed. Ruined. All that was once good is now stripped off by Satan.

Enyd's gaze follows theirs, finds the rifles. She takes two strides to the wall and picks up one of the weapons, but leaves the barrel pointing toward the stone floor. She takes a calm step toward the boys. Oliver and Thomas back toward the stairs, eyes locked on Enyd's gun.

Enyd. Stop.

She blocks Margaret from seeing through her eyes. From listening in. It's just her and the boys. The violence loving, bored out of their minds, boys.

"Enyd, please. Let's talk this through. I mean…" Oliver chuckles a bit, lowers his hands. "Do you even know how to use that thing?"

She slides the rifle's bolt back and then thrusts it forward, chambering a round. The assured movement, the uncharacteristic way she handles the gun sends Oliver's hands right back into the air. The rifle's ready to fire but still pointed at the floor.

With his voice lowered, Thomas whispers to Oliver, "Holy fuck. I guess she—"

Enyd lifts the barrel, aims it at Thomas' head, fires the rifle. Multiple screams echo from the basement room. The loud bang leaves Enyd's ears ringing. Thomas's body collapses onto the stairs.

Enyd slides the bolt back, thrusts it forward. Oliver backs away from her, tries to run but stumbles over Thomas's limp legs, which are blocking his escape. Enyd takes a step toward the boy.

"All this time. I thought the Beast was inside my head. In my chest. My blood. But no. It's been here, with you. Lurking. Sneaking. Molesting. Right under my eyes."

She aims the barrel at Oliver's head. Enyd lifts her chin and fingers the trigger gently. "You've lost your place in the heavenly paradise. You and that filth, lying next to you. But you won't take baby Samuel from me. I will save him. If it's the last thing I do."

The rifle's second bang stops the ringing in her ears.

It stops the screams. When the second body falls limp on the stairs, Enyd doesn't hear the thump. She's gone deaf to all sounds. Deaf to all that once connected her with this earthly reality.

CHAPTER 5
AFTERGLOW

Her head hurting and her ankles barely keeping her upright after climbing over the two dead bodies, Enyd collapses on the top stair. She's left the two corpses where her rifle dropped them. There's no one to pick them up. To drag the sinners upstairs and out of Kinship Care. The only ones strong enough to do so would be, well, the boys themselves.

Enyd needs to get that door open. She needs to reason with Hannah, tell her that once the baby arrives, it will belong with Enyd. Once the baby is up here with her, she'll know what to do. The baby. Their savior. Samuel's return. It'll all be clear then. If only Enyd knew anything about giving birth, about babies. Hannah might be too weak when the time comes. Is baby Samuel in danger? She needs a new plan, needs to be prepared. If only there was a nurse she could talk to—

Enyd forces herself back to her feet. Her ankles are on fire. Her body's sore and tired, but a new hope—a new plan—gives her the strength to take a step, and then another, and then a third, toward the library and finally her office.

The drawer is still open. Inside, most of the granola bars and root beers are gone. Margaret needed them to bribe the boys to take her side.

Enyd sits on the wooden chair and rummages through the drawer. Way down between the empty soda cans, Twinkies wrappers, and remaining granola bars, a red light blinks. The second set of AR-glasses. The ones Enyd has not yet crushed like a sinner's fingertip.

She grabs the AR-set and puts it on. The trailer flashes in front of her eyes. Smiling Beasts jogging. Shopping. Consuming. Sinning.

"Arnie, call…" Enyd takes the glasses off and takes a long look at the smashed camera in the corner of the room.

"Shit, shit, shit." How does she initiate the call?

"Call Nurse Saarinen."

Nothing.

"City of Finland, ring ring."

The trailer goes on. The three dots don't appear on the screen.

"Just bloody call Nurse Saarinen and City of Finland! Initiate this fucking call!"

The three dots appear on the glowing red background. Enyd waits. But unlike every other time she's ever called, Nurse Saarinen doesn't pick up.

Enyd takes the set off, folds it, and places it inside

her chest pocket. Fine then. First, we open the door. Then, we talk to the nurse.

With her ankles and mind on fire, Enyd leaves the office. She'll get that damned door open if it's the last thing she does before redeeming her place in the heavenly paradise. Baby Samuel will be saved. The Lord's son must be protected from sinners. From the granola-nibbling, porridge-begging scavengers that are his biological parents.

Minutes. That's what it takes for Enyd to climb upstairs. The bedroom doors are shut. The house is quiet. Quieter than she remembers it ever being. It's the same thing downstairs: a hundred and twelve kids have tucked themselves in, without lunch or tea or questions asked. Margaret must have told them to do so.

"Good," Enyd mumbles, leaning against the railing. A door opens to her right. A familiar round face peeks out. Owena walks out and heads straight to Enyd. The little girl takes Enyd's hand and places something against her palm. Then she closes Enyd's fingers around it.

A granola bar. With chocolate chips. Enyd looks down at the girl. Owena gives her a careful smile and says, "Sister Margaret said we need to hold on to the bars. That they're all we have to eat now."

"Then why are you giving it to me?"

"Because I don't want you to be hungry, Sister Enyd."

The little girl walks back to her bedroom door.

Before she closes the door, she turns around. Her full, round eyes investigate Enyd's face. "Will the bad things go away soon, Sister Enyd? Did Arnie use a mind control machine too?"

Enyd stares at the girl. The AR-set starts buzzing against her chest pocket. She forgets the little girl, drops the granola bar on the wall-to-wall carpet, and fiddles with the glasses. The familiar red glow fills the screen, "Nurse Saarinen?" she says, her voice raspy and throat dry.

The line is quiet for a few seconds. Then a voice Enyd hasn't heard for a long time echoes through the invisible earpiece. "No, dear. It's Doctor Solomon."

Images of the drill, the chip, white hospital sheets, and Laura Solomon's friendly and motherly face flash through Enyd's mind. Why is the doctor calling her now?

"Are you alone, Enyd?"

Enyd leans against the upstairs railing with one hand, and with the other, she turns and focuses on the images behind the red glow. Her reality. Owena stares at her with her mouth open, eyes filled with horror.

"The bad things," she whispers and bangs the bedroom door shut. Multiple bangs follow as curious eyes escape back to their hiding places. In Owena's room, furniture is moved around and set against the door.

"I'm with the children, Doctor Solomon. But I need your help."

"That much I've gathered. Why don't you step away and find a more private place so we can have a nice, long chat? Would you like that, dear?"

Enyd's rubber-soled slippers stick in the mud. She abandons the footwear and continues across the yard in her bare feet, carrying a rolling pin in her hand. Unlike Nurse Saarinen's slightly nasal voice and words, Laura Solomon is hard to resist. The lies she tells. The support she offers.

"It was never our intention to leave you high and dry, Enyd. If your chipping procedure had succeeded, we'd have brought you to the City of Finland and kept you here until the cleaning was completed. Then you could have chosen to either return to the City of England or stay here with us. Your employer didn't mince words when he spoke of your skills. Sounds like you're one hell of a counsellor, Enyd."

"Sister. Sister Enyd."

"Ahh, yes. I was told it was your idea to control the kids with religion."

It wasn't. It had been the reverend's idea, but Enyd doesn't correct the doctor.

"I would have suggested karma and rabbit feet. Talismans do well in the City of Finland. I guess it's just the nature of humanity that people always believe in something higher than themselves. Let it be a Norse folk tale or a hairy keychain. Most of us need to believe there's something greater out there. But maybe we just need to understand that the greatest powers we can ever find are already within."

"You mean the chip?"

Doctor Solomon's laughter caresses Enyd's ears. It's too easy to like this woman. Too easy to stay quiet and focus on her calm, reassuring words. It's like a warm breeze from her past. From the time before Samuel.

"Your inner strength, Enyd. But the chip is part of it, sure. The Happiness-Program is created to lift us up so we can be the best versions of ourselves. When all you want is a warm bath, and all you have is a bucket filled with cold water… there's nothing wrong with creating an illusion of a bathtub with warm water and inviting bubbles. The Chipped are quite happy with what they've got. A safe and secure reality away from the chaos. Isn't that what we all want and need?"

Enyd nods, unsure if the doctor can see the gesture. Doctor Solomon hasn't turned the camera on.

"But no system is perfect. I've never claimed ours to be perfect either. Some people get restless. Some refuse to take their pills. Some wander to places where those with a chip were never meant to go. I've lost a lot of my people, Enyd. And it's all because of an Unchipped woman who spreads lies and poisons my people's minds. I believe that woman is now coming your way. Kaarina travels with a Chipped woman called Niina. Her daughter, Ava, is one of your students there in the school, isn't that right?"

Enyd stops and leans against the broken horse statue by the front gates. She sets the rolling pin down on the ground. In the distance, white boxes rest against a green-brown hill. The warm winter has finally started to kill off the grass.

"It's not a school. Just a home. The Lord's haven."

"But Ava is there with you?"

Enyd thinks of the girl with ten purple fingertips, locked into a basement room with Margaret, a boy, and his pregnant friend. She thinks of baby Samuel. Their savior.

"She's here. Yes."

"Excellent. We're sending a team right away. I was told that Kaarina travels with some Americans now. I'm not sure how that's possible or why they're here, but those who come from the green city are known to be heavily armed and extremely dangerous. But our team will eliminate this threat, Enyd. I need you to remain calm until they arrive. Just don't use that CS-key. Not until you see my team. They'll be wearing blue uniforms. Okay, dear?"

What is she to believe in? The red luminosity in her eyes? Solomon's smooth and fulfilling words? The Beast curing the plague? Enyd sits down on the horse statue's concrete base. On the ground, a piece of the sculpture—a horse leg—is partly buried in the muddy ground. Enyd turns her back on the limb. It reminds her of rolling pins and basement rooms.

"This team you're sending. Will they have a medic traveling with them?"

"What's that, dear?"

"Will there be a nurse?"

The line falls silent for a while. Doctor Solomon doesn't understand. She doesn't know about Baby Samuel.

"Are you hurt, dear? Or is it one of your students?"

Enyd shakes her head. What is she doing? Why would she trust the Beast to help her? Medics or not, it'd be foolish to trust Baby Samuel in the hands of evil. No—Hannah must stay in the basement until the baby is out. Doesn't matter if it takes months. She must be kept away from all evil.

"Never mind. It's just a scratch. I don't need a nurse. Or a team. Blessed be the Lord. My rock, who trains my hands for war. And my fingers for battle."

Enyd takes off the AR-set and throws it on the ground. She reaches for the rolling pin on the ground, still staring at the devilish device in front of her. Her hand gropes and fumbles. Nothing.

Something smashes hard against her leg. Enyd falls forward and hits her head against the base of the statue. Eyesight blurred, she pushes her hands against the wet ground. She starts to crawl, but a foot pushes her back down. The rolling pin falls, landing next to the AR-glasses.

"Open the. Gate. Enyd. You need to. Let us. Out."

"All I want is to save them," Enyd says, pressed against the ground. "That's all I ever wanted."

"Violence. And starvation. Is not going to. Save. Them."

The reverend's voice appears. *"Sister Margaret is right, Enyd. This is hardly what your friend Samuel represented. What his religion was about."*

"But the Bible—"

"The Bible has many meanings. It's more about how you read it. More about you, than the written word. Can you imagine Samuel ever hurting another human being?"

He would never. Samuel had been kind. Devoted.

"The reverend. Is right. Enyd. You lost. Your way."

"Unlock the CS-key and let the kids go, Enyd. The plague didn't kill this Kaarina or those who travel with her. This should tell you the city is safe. Let them go, Enyd. It's not too late to fix this. I want the Chip-Charity to excel more than anyone. But this is too much."

Enyd opens her eyes. Moving her head seems impossible.

"And you'll save him? You'll save Baby Samuel?"

Margaret and the reverend ponder her words. Margaret snaps out an answer first. "We will. Save. Samuel. Just open the. Gate."

She needs to decide between the Beast and the She-Devil. And she needs to do it fast.

"And how am I supposed to get to the gate? You broke my leg."

Margaret kneels down to investigate Enyd's injuries. At the same time, her intermittent words reach out for the people around them. Those who should be here and those who shouldn't. Margaret keeps the connection open for Enyd to hear. Enyd's head fills with Unchipped voices.

"Ava. Bring them. Out."

"You're doing the right thing, Enyd. God will forgive you for what you've done."

"We're coming out, Margaret. Is Kaarina nearby?"

"We're here, Ava. Just get this gate open."

Enyd opens her mouth again, but the words fail her. All she can do is watch. Watch the She-Devil walk to Kinship Care's gates, a shadow following right behind her. A man with broad shoulders and big, strong hands. He's the size of a mountain.

A young woman with thin, white hair and bulky winter clothing grabs onto the metal bars, trying to shake the gate. "Ava!" she yells, but there is no answer.

A man with dreadlocks tied in a knot. He's not dressed in winter clothes, not like the others. His dark skin stands out from his pale companions.

Another man dressed in a women's black and purple winter coat and matching pants investigates the CS-key, rattling it against the front gate.

A girl's bruised arms—Ava's arms—block her view. Enyd closes her eyes but is too weak to protect herself from the blows to come.

But Ava doesn't hit her. No one does.

Enyd keeps her eyes closed and folds her hands. A dozen sets of hands hold onto her.

"Okay, guys. If we lift at the same time, we'll be able to carry Sister Enyd to the gate. Are you ready?" Ava says.

"Look!" It's Owena's voice. Her little finger points

at the AR-glasses. "It's the machine that controls minds. Satan got to Sister Enyd!"

Margaret picks up the statue leg and the AR-glasses. "It's not. That. Simple. Owena."

"But we need to crush the devil."

"Owena, not now," Ava says. "We need to carry Sister Enyd to the gate. Okay? On the count of three. One. Two. Three."

And then she's flying. As Enyd floats across Kinship Care's front yard, the image of Samuel's smiling face flickers on her closed eyelids. It wipes away all other images, those that have haunted Enyd for such a long time. Bruises. Blood. Red digits on the wall. Blinking glasses and trailers. Only Samuel remains. Waiting for Enyd to join him.

And then the floating stops. Enyd sits down on the ground, her back resting against the metal gates. The CS-key's green light blinks next to her head. The She-Devil kneels down, her green eyes locking with Enyd's.

"Hello, Enyd. I'm so sorry it all came down to this."

When Enyd stays quiet, Margaret kneels down next to her. She places the rolling pin and the AR-glasses next to Enyd on the ground.

"She is. Badly. Hurt."

"The Chipped will come for her. Laura's probably already sent her team. We must hurry, Margaret. Markus and Bill here will get Hannah from the basement. We just need to get this gate open."

Enyd reaches for the CS-key. It's close enough. All

she needs to do is place her hand on it, and the gate is open. Her hand hovers and falls limp at her side. "I need to know that Samuel will be okay."

The She-Devil looks at Margaret. "What is she talking about?"

Shaking her head, Margaret kneels down next to Enyd. *I give you. My word.*

Enyd closes her eyes again, but the image of Samuel is gone. All she sees is a red glimmering.

Margaret takes Enyd's hand and folds it in her own. "Enyd. Please."

Eyes shut, the tears start flowing down Enyd's face. "I'll give you all the chocolate bars. You can have my office. The AR-glasses. Just don't let it get Samuel. Don't let the Beast take him away."

Margaret squeezes Enyd's hand, pressing it against her chest. *I will save. Him. If you. Open. This gate.*

When Margaret places Enyd's hand on the CS-key, she doesn't resist. The lock pops open, and the metal gates start sliding aside.

Ava slips through the gates and rushes to hug an older woman that has the same high cheekbones and sharp look in her eyes that Ava has. While Ava hugs her mother, the She-Devil and her flock enter Kinship Care. Enyd lets her body relax and fall against the wet ground. Margaret takes off her thick sweater, bundles it into a pillow, and places it underneath Enyd's head. The red, fuzzy fabric is ticklish against her cheek.

The lock-bundle and another man—the one with

the women's winter gear—start running toward the house. A barking terrier runs in circles, then sits between the Devil and her mountain.

A dog? Am I dreaming? Is this the end?

The She-Devil makes her way to the children. "Don't be afraid."Her voice is pleasant, like the creamy filling inside a Twinkie. "My name is Kaarina, and I've come to help you."

Don't believe her. Don't fall for it.

None of the children reply. Instead, they eye the man that stands next to the Devil-woman. She turns and points at the man, then waves him off. "You don't need to be afraid of him either," she says, chuckling happily. "At first, he might seem intimidating and rude. But at the end of the day, he's quite friendly. Like a gigantic and clumsy Yeti."

Some of the children giggle when they recognize the character from one of the library's fairy tale books. The story of a Yeti had been Owena's favorite. She steps closer and reaches for the She-Devil's hand.

"I'm Owena. This is Sarah and Marie. We are Ava's roommates."

"Hi, Owena. So nice to meet you. I know Ava's mother, and we've come to take her away. Would you like to come with us?"

"Away, where?"

The Devil turns on her muck boot heels. She points at the white boxes in the distance. "Well, first we're going to go open those presents and see if we can find you all some food. Then, your friend Margaret here will help you all walk all the way to…" The Devil's finger moves to point at the red glow on the horizon, "…there."

"But that's where evil lives."

"What makes you think that, Owena?" Kaarina says, surprise in her voice. "I've just come from there, and I can tell you that it's not all evil out there. Good people still remain in the city. Kind people. You just need to know where to look."

Enyd hears footsteps returning from the house. She forces her eyes open and sees Noah and the two strange men helping Hannah toward the open gate. A steady flow of children follow them across the yard—and out the metal gates.

Margaret kneels down next to Enyd. "Help. Is coming. I am. Sorry. Sister."

Baby Samuel is under that oversized sweater. He's being robbed from Enyd. From Samuel. From the Lord. Enyd watches hopelessly as everything she has left to live for gathers outside the gates to leave Kinship Care. To leave her.

Margaret squeezes Enyd's shoulder. Then she gets up and walks over to the She-Devil. She places her hand on the small of the Beast's back and turns her away from the children. Enyd opens her mouth to talk, but she's too drained by the agony and hurt to speak. It's hard to keep her eyes open.

"I know. People in. The city. Kaarina. I'll be. Safe."

"You work with the Chipped?"

"I used. To."

"Hannah needs to go to the hospital. She's bleeding. Can you take her?"

"I'll stay. With Hannah. You take. The rest with. You."

Side by side, Margaret walks with the She-Devil and the Yeti. The children follow them out of the gate. Some hold hands, some jump and dance happily outside the gate. Some whisper into each other's ears, pointing at the white boxes far in the distance. They clap their hands and squeal with joy.

Like a stream of ants, they cross the rolling hills. The line stops by the white boxes, where they fill their pockets and then continue forward—onto the field, up the rolling hills, and into the red glow.

Kinship Care falls quiet. The cold and wet ground feels like cement under Enyd's tired body. She reaches for the red sweater and spreads it over her body. Like a red flag in front of a bull's eyes, it will draw the Beast to her.

A few feet away from Enyd's head, she hears footsteps walking over to the AR-glasses. Too beat to open her eyes, Enyd hears something rustling against the ground. Then, a sharp cracking sound sends plastic flying. Pieces of the AR-glasses land in Enyd's hair.

There's movement on Enyd's left side. Small feet appear.

"Sister Enyd?"

A warm wave of relief washes over Enyd's body.

Owena. She's left herself behind. She must have been hiding behind the statue all this time. She refuses to join the She-Devil. Refuses to abandon the one who's taken care of her all these years. Owena doesn't care about the treats inside the white boxes. Or fairy tales about the Yeti. More than the hunger in her tummy or her fear of evil—she cares about Enyd.

Enyd opens her mouth. She forces the words out. "Owena, sweetheart. You came—"

As Enyd finally opens her eyes, the words freeze on her blue lips as she sees the little girl holding a rolling pin. Owena takes a step closer and raises the weapon above her head. "Bad things control minds," she says. "Satan took you over, Sister Enyd. With the glasses. But don't worry. I know what to do." Her hands shake slightly as she moves closer.

Owena swings the rolling pin hard into Enyd's head. Her ears are ringing, and the taste of metal wells up in her mouth. The Beast will find her body, beaten and crushed. But that's okay. Laura Solomon's team will carry her into a black SUV and try to save her brain. Let them.

Now, Enyd doesn't have to decide. There's no one left for her to save. No doomed sinners for her to rescue. Half-smiling, she enjoys the sensation of earth, swallowing her, lulling her into nothingness. How good it feels to let go. Not to be the one holding the reins.

Owena grunts beside her. Still smiling, Enyd keeps her eyes closed while the girl smashes the rolling pin against Enyd's skull. Another hit lands on her face. And another. Enyd drifts further and further away, images of rolling pins and AR-glasses flashing through her drained mind. Just before the darkness closes in, she hears Owena's stern words.

"I know how to crush the devil, Sister Enyd. I know because you showed me."

EPILOGUE

Stacks of mildewed paper, mountains of ransacked clothing, kitchenware, and bedsheets fill the cluttered, spacious living room. Or what used to be a living room. Margaret's home. Margaret has sat down on a wobbly office chair, her fingers frozen on the writing desk. Staring into space, she's been zoned out for a while. Ava's fingers grip a dead smartphone. Back in Kinship Care, she hadn't thought to grab a charger. Instead she had stuffed her pockets full of Enyd's chocolate chip bars and a phone that belonged to her in the first place. The lack of battery doesn't bother Ava. She's with her mother now. With the other Unchipped—running away from those who hunt her kind.

"Margaret, we really need to get going," Kaarina says next to Ava. "Hannah is in a lot of pain." But the woman stays in her frozen state. Kaarina looks at Ava, pleading. She's right. Hannah should be at the hospital already.

Ava walks to a half-burned pile of things from

Margaret's previous life. While she's been away, someone has used Margaret's belongings to build a bonfire. Ava picks up a broken picture frame, but only a blackened strip of photo paper remains. Did Margaret live here alone? If not, where is her family now? Ava has so many questions. But Margaret sits with her back to the rest of them. Her mind occupied, stuck somewhere in her past, she can't turn around and read Ava's lips.

Ava could tap her, snap her out of it with this new ability she's been introduced to. But maybe the deaf woman doesn't want Ava peeking into her past. Maybe Ava wouldn't like what she'd see.

Kaarina walks into the room. A man with shoulders so broad he needs to turn sideways to fit through the doors is carrying a black trash bag, filled with things they've picked up around the apartment. Toothpaste, soap, clothing, towels, bandages, and Betadine. The Yeti turns to Kaarina and leans in to talk to her. When Kaarina whispers, the man leaves the room.

"Hannah is barely hanging on," Kaarina says, her eyes fixed on Margaret's back. "Does the car in the garage work? Are you able to drive it to the city?"

Ava kneels down and sets the empty picture frame back into the bonfire. A porcelain hand pokes out from the ashes. A doll. Her glass eyes stare into Ava's. *Who did you belong to? Did Margaret have a daughter?* Of course, the toy can't answer her tapping. But suddenly Ava must know more about the woman who she's lived with for the past two years. The woman who saved them all from the Charity program.

"Margaret? Yeti saw a drone in the distance. We're running out of time."

Kaarina's words bring Margaret's hands back to life. Nodding repeatedly, she reaches to the back of the writing desk, runs her fingers on its wooden surface. With a sharp *click,* the desk's top slides open, revealing a hidden drawer. Margaret reaches in and fishes out an old-fashioned laptop. Placing the device under her armpit, she picks out a charger and a small, metallic object. A memory stick.

Margaret hurries to Kaarina. "Take it. Use it. But don't try. To fight them. Bring the kids. To safety."

"But there's over a hundred of them."

"I know."

Kaarina investigates Margaret's face. When she finds no trace of doubt there, Kaarina opens the laptop's lid. "Is there a password? A code?"

Margaret nods. "RESORT. That will. Let you. In. Change it. To something. Safer."

"And then what?"

"You'll find a. Map."

"A map? To a safe place?"

"For. Now. And once. Those who you. Trust the most. Turn against. You. Open the. File."

"Who will turn against me? Margaret, I don't like riddles."

Margaret walks back to the desk and clicks the hidden drawer shut. Then her eyes spot something in the bonfire's remains. A metal jewelry box. She picks it up, opens it, and takes something out. A gold cross necklace. Ava holds her breath when Margaret walks to her and hangs the chain around Ava's neck. She takes Ava's hand and places the memory stick in it, then closes Ava's fingers into a fist.

"The file. Opens with. A code only. Ava knows."

"Me? I don't know any codes or passwords, Sister... I mean, Margaret."

Margaret gives her a hug, then holds Ava by the shoulders. Then Margaret's soft voice booms inside Ava's head. *It's the. Same code. That opened. Enyd's drawer.*

But Enyd was terrible. Why should we trust anything she created?

"Enyd wasn't. Evil, Ava. She got lost. She misunderstood. Got scared. Besides the. Drawer. Was never. Enyd's. In the first. Place."

It was yours? You were in charge of the Charity—

"What is this, Margaret?" Kaarina's words interrupt their silent conversation. The laptop's blue light reflects against her pale face. Her eyes move on the screen fast, reading, soaking it all in. Her teeth bite into her mud and blood covered thumbnail. "So, it was planted in the drinking water? The plague?"

Margaret pets Ava's cheek, gets up, and walks to the front door.

"Don't drink. From the faucets. Do not. Shower. Just follow the. Map. And get out. Of here."

Ava runs to Margaret and reaches for her hand.

"Wait, you're not coming with us? Once Hannah is in the hospital? What if they hurt you, the Chipped?"

Margaret turns around. Without looking into her eyes, she gives Ava one more careful smile. Something dark shadows her weary face.

"They won't. Hurt. One of. Their own."

Shoot! Book 3 of the Unchipped story is at a close. But don't worry, you can find out what happens next in <u>Book 4 in the Unchipped series, UNCHIPPED: Luna available on Amazon</u>

My dearest reader,

You are simply amazing! Thank you so much for your support and readership! I can't tell you how much you reading this book means to me. I'm humbled and honored that you've dedicated your valuable time to experience the Unchipped universe with me. I'm still a newbie author, so if you were to leave me a review on Amazon it would be a huge help! Short or long, doesn't matter. Reviews are the best way to help other readers find the Unchipped Series.

Want to stay in touch? I would love it if you'd subscribe to my newsletter:

@ www.TayaDeVere.com/HappinessProgram

Starting in August 2020, newsletter subscribers will receive free, exclusive early access to in-universe short stories from the Unchipped series a week before each book comes out. That's every eighteen days so be sure to sign up to get first crack at the series!

Facebook – facebook.com/tayadevereauthor
Instagram – instagram.com/tayadevere_author
Goodreads – goodreads.com/tayadevere
Bookbub – bookbub.com/authors/taya-devere
Amazon – amazon.com/Taya-DeVere/e/B07KRJPMTV

Gratefully yours,
Taya DeVere

THE END

About the Author

Taya is a Finnish-American author, writing contemporary fiction and dystopian sci-fi. After living and traveling in America for seven years, she now lives in Finland with her husband Chris, their dog Seamus, three bunny-boys (Ronin, Baby, Loki), and her horse of a lifetime, Arabella.

Best things in life: friends & family, memories made, and mistakes to learn from. Taya also loves licorice ice cream, secondhand clothes and things, bunny sneezes, salmiakki, and sauna.

Dislikes: clowns, the Muppets, Moomin trolls, dolls (especially porcelain dolls), human size mascots and celery.

Taya's writing is inspired by the works of authors like Margaret Atwood, Peter Heller, Hugh Howey, and C.M. Martens.

Final Thanks

A free spirit. An odd duck. Someone who refuses to go with the flow. I've been called these, among many other things, over the years. To many, my choices and plans (or lack of) have rarely made much sense. But I grew up not caring how other people see me. I've always chosen my own path, even when it meant that I wouldn't fit in.

And it's all thanks to my parents.

My father was a strong, confident person. When he walked into a room, everyone would notice. Not because he was loud or obnoxious, but because of his strong presence. Okay—he *was* loud *and* obnoxious sometimes. But ask anyone who once knew him, and they'll tell you that without fail, he was truly and authentically himself throughout his life. During his career, he created a famous slogan that most people in Finland would recognize even today. "*Vain pakki puuttuu.*" It's a slogan for a bicycle company, and it means "Only missing a reverse." This is who he was.

And this is the kind of person he taught me to be. Never look back, always go forward. Even if you're scared shitless and shaking in your boots.

Thank you, *iskä*, for teaching me to be brave enough to be myself.

When she was young, my mother wasn't dealt the best cards in life. Pain, suffering, doubt, and heartache were present in her life since the day she was born. Still, somehow, she made it. Alone and without anyone's help, she moved away from Finland, traveled across the globe, and started a new life. One night, after three years of working and living in Israel, she happened to meet a Finnish soldier on the streets of her hometown. This young soldier asked mom if he could buy her a drink.

She said no.

But stubborn as he was, my dad wouldn't take no for an answer. And, so the story goes, my mom agreed to have "just one drink" with him. Boy, am I glad she did!

Thank you, *äiti*, for teaching me to do the right thing, ever since I was knee-high. Thank you for putting up with my shenanigans when I was a clueless teen. Thank you for letting me go when I decided to move across the pond when I was twenty-something. And thank you for never judging me for my thoughts, my (sometimes terrible) ideas, and my beliefs.

Thank you both for helping me become the person I am today.

The Unchipped series – Release schedule 2020
UNCHIPPED: KAARINA - 8/31/2020
UNCHIPPED: WILLIAM - 9/18/2020
UNCHIPPED: ENYD - 10/6/2020
UNCHIPPED: LUNA - 10/24/2020
UNCHIPPED: THE RESORT - 11/11/2020
~~UN~~CHIPPED: LAURA - 11/30/2020
~~UN~~CHIPPED: DENNIS - 12/18/2020

CPSIA information can be obtained
at www.ICGtesting.com
Printed in the USA
LVHW031745220920
666797LV00013B/1781